CURSED MAGIC
CLEARWATER WITCHES #5

Madeline Freeman

For information:

http://www.madelinefreeman.net

Cursed Magic — Clearwater Witches, Book 5

ISBN: 1530469260
ISBN-13: 978-1530469260

ACKNOWLEDGMENTS

Thank you Steven Novak for the fabulous cover.

Thanks to Leah at Invisible Ink Editing for your assistance in polishing this novel.

Chapter One
Krissa

The promise of summer hangs heavy in the halls of Clearwater High. All around me, my fellow students' eyes are gleaming with the kind of manic glint I always associate with upcoming exams. The school year is almost over, and I can't believe how much has changed since it began. New school, new timeline.

New boyfriend.

Owen Marsh keeps pace beside me, his fingers laced with mine. Just weeks ago, I was convinced I couldn't be with him, that I was no good for him, but things have changed. More than ever, I've realized how much we need each other. I pulled away from him once, positive that any interaction would hurt him, but he made me see that pulling away was what did damage. I've vowed to be honest with him, no matter what, and he's promised to help me through any challenge. Our lives may never be perfect, but at least we'll have each other.

As we walk, he chats about plans for reviewing for the final in our shared sixth-hour class. With Owen beside me and summer ahead, things couldn't be better.

I rub the pad of my thumb absently against the band of the ring on my right hand. Well, maybe things could be a little better. But, so far, the spell keeping me tethered to my true self is holding.

Mostly.

Walking down the hall in the opposite direction are Fox

Holloway and Dana Crawford. Her hand curls around his bicep somewhat possessively, but she smiles when she catches my eye. She's been much warmer toward me since the night of the Influence spell, but I suppose that's to be expected. Because of me, the psychic abilities she wanted so badly are once again hers. I gave her mine to save her from a darker fate. To make sure she wouldn't be filled with the darkness she and Crystal Jamison summoned.

My gaze flickers to Fox, and I offer him a smile. The corners of his mouth upturn, but there's a hardness in his eyes. He's been distant with me since he learned—from Dana—how Crystal and I altered the timeline, how I'm not the same girl he dated for three years. There was a moment—right after the Influence spell—when I thought he might be able to forgive me for lying, but in the last few weeks, he's gone back to acting strange around me. I sigh. Maybe one day he and I can be friends again.

"Here's your stop," Owen says as the warning bell rings. "I'll see you after class."

"Yeah, I'll see you." My heart flutters as he leans in close for a kiss. No matter how many times his lips brush mine, I still get butterflies like it's the first. What I wouldn't give to be able to leave the school day behind and spend the rest of the afternoon like this with Owen.

"Not again." Mr. Martin's voice cuts through my happy little bubble. "I thought I warned you two already."

Owen pulls away and I miss his closeness immediately. He offers a sheepish grin and a little salute. "Mr. Martin." He winks at me before starting toward his own classroom.

Mr. Martin's eyes bore a hole into me as I skirt past him into the room. "I understand it's almost the end of the year, but that doesn't mean the rules no longer apply, Miss Barnette. If you refresh yourself on the code of conduct in your student planner, you'll see that public displays of affection are strictly prohibited."

His voice follows me as I attempt to make my way to my seat. He must be in a bad mood; usually he doesn't give me this much grief.

"Stop and look at me when I'm talking to you," he snaps. "Show a little respect. What is it with parents these days not teaching their children how to respect authority?"

I don't want to, but I stop and turn. I know him well enough to be sure that if I don't, he'll spend the first half of class on a tirade on the subject. "I'm sorry, Mr. Martin."

He crosses his thick arms across his stout trunk. His face is red—from the heat of the room or his anger, I'm not sure. "This may be hard for you to believe, but your apology doesn't mean much. This isn't the first time I've warned you about PDAs with your boyfriend. If you were really sorry, you'd actually change your behavior."

Red tinges my periphery. I start in on the breathing exercises I've been using to calm myself. Inhale. Hold. Exhale slowly. Repeat. The bell rings overhead, signaling the start of class, but Mr. Martin ignores it. Instead, he continues on about my lack of respect. I want him to shut up—I *need* him to shut up. The eyes of my classmates prickle my skin. The usual pre-class chatter dies down as everyone tunes in to the entertainment up front.

More red smoke swirls around, encroaching further on my vision. My deep breathing trick isn't working. A crackle, like electricity, surges just beneath my skin. I flex my fingers in an attempt to rid them of the itching sensation building there.

I can't give in. I can't let the Influence take control.

Mr. Martin opens his mouth again to continue outlining what a disrespectful child I am, but his words don't make it out. In a flash, my left arm slashes through the air and Mr. Martin's head flies off his body, landing with a wet splat at the feet of a blonde girl in the first row. The room goes silent for a moment, but as Mr. Martin's body crumples lifelessly to the floor, the room erupts in screams of terror. Those closest to the door run for it, while those nearest to me dart toward the back of the room and press themselves against the wall. Blood from the jagged flesh at the end of Mr. Martin's neck oozes around my feet.

Someone tugs at my arm. "Krissa?" Crystal Jamison asks tentatively.

I close my eyes and the red dissipates. When I open them, Mr. Martin is standing there, whole and unharmed, staring at me as if I'm an idiot.

"Yes, please, Miss Jamison. Will you escort your friend to her desk so I can start class? Apparently she's incapable of finding it on her own."

"Of course," Crystal murmurs, her stone-blue eyes locked on my face as she hooks her hand in the crook of my arm.

"I won't hesitate to suspend students," Mr. Martin mutters darkly as Crystal leads me up the aisle. "Even if it's almost finals. I can't imagine Miss Tanner would have any qualms about granting my request..."

I do my best to tune out his droning voice as I slide into my desk. Bridget Burke tilts her head and squints at me. "You okay? You, like, totally zoned up there."

The image of Mr. Martin's head flopping to the ground flashes in my mind's eye, but I quickly stuff it down. I don't want to think about it.

I rub the hemp bracelet on my wrist. It's woven with small chunks of Apache tears and snowflake obsidian. When I made it months ago, it was to keep others from picking up on my thoughts—to keep them from seeing the darkness inside me. It's almost laughable now. I had no idea then what real darkness was.

It was Anya's idea for me to continue wearing the bracelet. She was afraid the Influence might try to affect other people in my life since the enchantment on my ring keeps it from getting a firm grip on me. At the time, I thought she was being overly cautious, but now I'm thankful for an excuse to keep it on. If the psychics *could* peer into my mind, they would see how much harder it's becoming to ignore the Influence.

But neither Bridget nor Crystal is psychic. They couldn't read my thoughts even if they tried. I pin a smile on my face, hoping it doesn't look too forced. "Yeah. I guess I did kind of space." I cast my thoughts back to the moments before I entered the classroom. My smile softens as Owen's face fills my memory. "Owen kissed me in the hall."

Bridget rolls her eyes, but her silly grin is enough to assure me she's buying my explanation. "You think you'd be used to it by now. All you guys do is suck face." She pokes her tongue through her lips before turning her attention to the front of the room. Mr. Martin is calling for the class's attention.

Dutifully, I fix my gaze in the teacher's direction, but my skin prickles again. Crystal's still watching me. I wish I could read her mind—but those days are behind me. Even without the ability to peek into Crystal's thoughts, though, I'm pretty sure she doesn't believe me. She was up there next to me, and I'm fairly certain I didn't look blissed out from kissing my boyfriend when she grabbed my arm.

It's not until Mr. Martin directs us to pull out our textbooks that Crystal looks away. I use the moment to sneak my phone from my back pocket and type out a quick text: *It's getting worse.*

Chapter Two
Brody

The high priestess's fane is a thing of beauty. I've always loved the look of the white-sided colonial-style house that serves as the office of the Amaranthine leader. Its elegance and grace is lacking in most architectural designs of the last quarter century or so. But then, this house is older than that.

When I enter, I veer to the right instead of immediately climbing the stairs that are almost directly in front of me. I want to check my appearance one final time before meeting with Jade Barry, and I won't make the rookie mistake of inspecting my teeth in the mirror on the landing between the first and second floors. I learned years ago about how that mirror is enchanted to connect to a smaller mirror in the priestess's office. She and I have laughed many times about the social faux pas committed by unknowing Amaranthine in front of that mirror.

I spend less than a minute in front of the other mirror, and I'm glad I stopped. Jade has a sharp eye and definitely would have noticed the fleck of lint on the shoulder of my pressed navy button-down.

When I ascend the stairs, I do so slowly, purposefully, and flash a smile into the large gilt mirror on the landing. The carved details around the edges are superb. I've always appreciated the craftsmanship. This mirror was hand-selected by Jade and has been here for nearly twenty-five years. Every new priest or priestess chooses the looking glass that rests here.

I've already got mine picked out.

A smile tugs at the corner of my mouth. It's not that I don't respect Jade—I do. I even like her. But I've been waiting years for her term to be up; I'm certain of my place as next in line to succeed her. It's hardly written law, but in the last century, every new high priest or priestess has first filled the role of chief liaison. Jade herself held the position before I took over. She's been grooming me for decades.

The upstairs of the fane is as ornately decorated as the first floor, but the style is dated. The pastel colors hearken to a different decade, and the style of the decorative touches come from an even more distant time. Try as I might, I can't help redecorating in my mind as I approach the room on my right. The door is open and I smile as I poke my head in. "Good afternoon."

Phoebe, Jade's assistant, flushes at the sound of my voice. She always does. While it's customary for a new leader to bring in his own staff, more than once I've considered keeping Phoebe on as my assistant, simply because I have this effect on her. "Mr. Ford. Hello," she trills breathlessly.

"How many times do I have to tell you—it's Brody. Calling me Mr. Ford only makes me feel old." I wink and she giggles. In fact, I *am* old by most people's standards: I'll be seventy-seven in the fall. Not that the average person would know that from looking at me. I've been told by several that I don't look older than my mid-twenties. One of the many perks of being a member of the Amaranthine. I still have decades ahead of me, and I'll never look as old as most ordinary people do by my age.

"Is she in her office?"

Phoebe nods. "You can go right in."

I offer a final wink before starting for the door at the end of the hall. In another time, this would have been the master bedroom, but now it serves as Jade's office. I tap on the door before opening it. Inside, Jade sits behind a large, ornately carved mahogany desk. I can't help eyeing the leather chair she sits in, weighing the pros and cons of keeping it when this is my office. I've always liked the desk, so it will definitely stay.

As Jade's eyes flick to me, I put my redecorating plans on hold and cross to the smaller leather chair on the side of the desk nearest me. Jade looks as polished as ever: Her dark brown hair falls in gentle waves around her shoulders, and her nails perfectly match the carmine dress she wears. I offer a smile, fully expecting one in return. Jade and I have always been on good terms. But Jade's full lips don't curl. Instead, her eyes narrow and she tilts her chin up imperiously.

"Thank you for joining me, Brody." Her voice is formal. Cold.

"Of course," I say, injecting a measure of confidence into my tone. In all the years I've known her—it's been more than a few— I've never seen this look on her face. At least, I've never seen it directed at me. "What can I do for you?"

Jade exhales heavily and leans back into her plush chair. "I think it's time you and I have a serious conversation about your failing in Clearwater."

The words hit me like a sucker punch. I've spent nearly two months trying to put Clearwater out of my mind. What I expected would be a simple intelligence-gathering mission turned out to be more complicated than anticipated. But despite the challenges, I succeeded. "I got the information—the words Bess Taylor spent so many generations waiting to tell us. I'd hardly call that a failing."

"You *claim* to have gotten the information." She tilts her head, daring me to disagree.

I have half a mind to. I was there; I watched Crystal Jamison cast the spell that allowed her to contact her long-dead relative. I have no reason to believe she was deceitful. She would've told me anything I wanted to know to ensure her family's safety.

Before I can mount a defense, however, Jade continues. "You

also managed to get our assassin killed."

This pronouncement I can't accept. "Kai's death was his own fault. He'd faced deadlier foes before. How could I have known a group of teenagers would be able to get the drop on him?" I cross my arms over my chest. I'm not attempting to cover up the facts. Everything I've said is the truth.

From the look on Jade's face, she doesn't share my assessment. "Never in the history of the Amaranthine have we been as vulnerable as we are now."

I snort. The idea of the Amaranthine as weak is ludicrous. While we haven't yet attained immortality, we've come as close as anyone can. The spells we work don't just extend our lives far beyond their natural length; they increase our vitality and strengthen our magic. When a person reaches an age when the longevity enchantments will no longer take, he goes through the releasing ceremony. Instead of his powers being absorbed back into nature, they're directed to the remaining Amaranthine. "I wouldn't say we're vulnerable. Name me a coven with half the power we have."

Jade arches an eyebrow. "Circle Sica, the Biyacaré, Clan Twilight..."

It's unsettling how easily the names roll off her tongue. I've heard them before, of course, but I've never considered them a threat. Circle Sica typically keep to themselves in the Canadian wilderness. They don't play well with more civilized witches, but they rarely have the occasion to interact with them. The Biyacaré are shrewd in business and unforgiving when it comes to breaking deals, but they haven't left Europe in my lifetime. Clan Twilight are the only domestic threat. The Amaranthine have a longstanding treaty with them that holds so long as neither group passes into the other's territory. "Come on, Jade, you can't honestly think any of them could stand against us."

"Ordinarily, I'd agree with you. But without an assassin, we're in danger. You need to be able to see that, Brody. You need to know

9

how to anticipate threats. That you can't is one of your greatest weaknesses."

I shift in my seat. It's been decades since someone has tried to convince me I have flaws. In fact, Jade is usually one of the ones building me up. I don't like the idea that she's scrutinizing me now for the areas I'm left wanting. "Where are we in training a new assassin?"

Jade rubs her forehead absently. "That's not the way it works. I would've thought you knew that."

I clench my teeth, angry at myself for revealing another fault. If I'm honest, I've never paid much attention to how the assassin is chosen. The position isn't one that engenders respect—only fear. The role also doesn't change hands often, because any assassin worth the title is able to keep himself alive for decades. I cast my mind back to the time before Kai took the title. "Kai had to kill the last one. That's how he proved he was ready to protect us." I lift my hands. "Well, there's no one left to kill, so I suppose the next person in line can just take over. Is there something I'm missing?"

Jade narrows her eyes as she studies me. "Perhaps it was before your time, but Kai didn't become the assassin simply by merit of killing the last person to do the job. There were omens surrounding his birth. The darkness lived inside him from an early age. We knew what it meant, and we honed it, sharpened it. Before he was old enough to realize what we were doing, we were training him to be a killer, to be ruthless. That's how it's always been. We've always had a second in line to take over. But there've been no omens. There's no one waiting to take his place. We're honestly at a loss for what to do now."

The hairs on the back of my neck stand up as the implication of her words sinks in. Kai wasn't supposed to die in Clearwater. If he was, there would have been another ready to take his place. Perhaps things aren't as simple as I've been assuming.

Jade is eyeing me shrewdly. I do my best not to show how

uncomfortable the news has made me. "I trust you have the best minds working on that problem," I say, hoping to close the discussion. I need to spin this, to control the damage. I need her to see this information as something that could be positive. "Have you considered we may not need an assassin if we can follow Bess's instructions? Once we're immortal, we'll be invulnerable. Maybe that's why we don't have a new assassin lined up—perhaps we won't need one."

She surveys me for a long moment as if weighing whether or not to tell me something else. I don't like it one bit; I've been privy to her secrets for decades. "We're no closer to immortality than we were before your visit to Clearwater."

My muscles tense. I can't believe what she's saying. We've spent countless years searching for the words Bess Taylor wasn't able to share before her untimely death. My whole life I've been led to believe that once we knew her secret, we'd finally achieve the eternal life she sought. "How can you say that? We know what we've been waiting to hear. How can that leave us no closer?"

She ignores my incredulous tone, her face impassive. "We haven't been able to substantiate the information you brought back: 'The midnight stone must be imbued with the power of deepest night.' We have no idea what this midnight stone is, and we don't know what the 'power of deepest night' is supposed to mean." She sighs, and for the first time, she seems old. Nothing about her physical appearance changes, but her vitality seems to decrease. "The lack of actionable information coupled with the death of our assassin leaves me wishing you'd never traveled to Clearwater in the first place."

In my mind, I defend myself: I was just there to gather intelligence. We have people who are supposed to know the ins and outs of magic as well as they know how to breathe. That's not my job—not my area. But if I say all of that, I don't imagine it will win me any favors. The high priest must be informed about all such matters. I can't appear flip or unconcerned. So I take in a steadying breath, but before I can speak, the door to the office bangs open.

I spin in my chair, ready to tell the intruder to leave, but I stop short. I recognize the woman taking quick strides into the room: Her name is Lena Wiley. She's young—only around thirty although, like all of us, she looks younger—but she's already made a name for herself. Despite holding no position of power as an assistant researcher, she has a reputation for being tenacious and fiery, someone who doggedly goes after a problem. Her build is thin and slight, and she looks as if she could be taken down by a stiff breeze. Her long, dark brown hair is pulled into a sleek ponytail at the base of her neck. Besides a touch of gloss on her lips, the only other makeup she wears is thick, black eyeliner around her striking green eyes.

I glare at her. No matter how much of a spitfire this girl is, she has to know it's bad form to enter into the high priestess's presence unsummoned and unannounced.

Lena's eyes slide to me for a brief moment before fixing on Jade. "I'm sorry for barging in," she says, approaching Jade's desk.

I sit back, waiting for Jade to yell, to point, to send Lena away for being so presumptuous, but Jade does none of those things. A politely puzzled look crosses her face, and she nods. "Proceed."

"I think I know what midnight stone is," she says, approaching the desk. She stands close to my chair, despite the fact that there is plenty of room between it and the matching one to my left. "It's a mineral. The proper name is carcinite. It's very, very rare, found only in meteorites that come from deep space. It doesn't exist naturally on Earth, which is probably why it was so hard to track down. The only samples on the planet come from meteor strikes— and I've been able to locate them."

"This is excellent news," Jade says. She presses her hands against the desktop and stands. "I'll dispatch a team right away to go—"

Lena shakes her head. "It's not going to be that easy. You won't like where I found it."

I cross my arms over my chest. Is she trying to be dramatic on purpose, or does she think so little of Jade's time? "And do you feel like sharing?"

Jade tsks, which rankles me. There's need for her to scold me like a child. "Where is it?" she asks.

Lena smooths her dark hair against her head. "Clan Twilight. I'm not sure what their interest is, but I doubt they'll want to part with it."

Jade sucks in a breath. "There's no way we can take them on right now. Not with our... present limitations."

At this, Lena brightens. "If you like, I could write up a list of possible candidates for assassin. I understand we typically find them in-house, but since there have been no omens, maybe we can find someone on the outside."

A smile curves Jade's lips. Her eyes flash as they settle on Lena, taking in her tailored button-down shirt, pencil skirt, and kitten heel shoes. I don't like the way Jade's looking at her—like she's found a shiny new toy.

It's the way she used to look at me.

"I'll admit, I've been considering searching outside our ranks for a new assassin. I'm thankful there's someone like you to take the initiative to locate some candidates."

Lena grins broadly. "I can get you some names by this afternoon, if you like."

I can't stand for this. My mind spins as it attempts to draw the spotlight from this girl, this usurper. She's going out of her way to impress Jade. I can't risk Jade's respect switching to someone else—not when we're this close to her stepping down as our leader. "That won't be necessary," I say, bringing the attention back to myself. When Jade's eyes fix on me, a muscle in Lena's jaw jumps. She doesn't like that I'm stealing her thunder, but I don't care. I don't know what her motives are, but I won't stand idly by and watch her win Jade's affection. "There's no need to compile a list when I already know the perfect person for the job."

"Don't leave us in suspense," Jade says. Her tone indicates she's not sure I can deliver on my promise. I don't blame her, because I'm not sure I can either.

My mind spins. I don't actually have a candidate in mind—I just can't stand the thought of Lena solving another problem. I don't know what kinds of omens are associated with a new assassin—but that doesn't matter anyway, since Jade said there haven't been any. But the final bit of proof needed before someone claims the role is for the candidate to kill the current assassin, and there is one person who has fulfilled that requirement already. "Krissa Barnette. She's perfect. Jade, you said we usually have to train our assassins to be ruthless. We won't need to do that with her. Since she took on the Influence, the ruthlessness should come easily. We'll just have to direct her."

I pause, waiting for a reaction. When none comes, I add, "She's the one who killed Kai. She's already proven her abilities."

A smile spreads itself across Jade's face. "I hadn't even thought of that. Maybe something good will come from your visit to Clearwater after all."

Lena glares as if there's nothing she'd like better than to punch me in the face. "In case that doesn't work, I could still curate a list."

Jade shakes her head. "That won't be necessary. Thank you for your help, Miss Wiley."

I do my best not to smirk as Lena turns toward the door. Obviously, this meeting didn't end the way she intended. She spares only one glance in my direction before exiting the room, and the fire in her eyes makes it clear she won't be giving up easily.

When the door closes, Jade settles back behind her desk. "Well, Brody, you may be able to make up for the messy business in Clearwater after all. It seems our two big problems have been boiled down to one. We need an assassin for protection, but we also need one so we can get the carcinite from Clan Twilight."

I stand and draw my shoulders back. "I'll leave for Clearwater soon. She has friends who might try to stand in the way of her coming back with me, but I'll make sure they're not obstacles."

Jade nods, locking her eyes on mine. "Make your plans, but don't wait too long."

She doesn't say goodbye, but it's obvious I've been dismissed. I bow my head in respect before striding toward the door. Part of the reason she doesn't want me to wait is for the sake of our people, but I can't help wondering if another part has to do with her term ending soon. If I'm unable to deliver on my promise, there's no way she will endorse me to take over her role when she steps down. And if she doesn't endorse me, there's little chance I'll become the next Amaranthine leader.

I have to get to Clearwater soon. I hope this trip goes smoother than the last.

Chapter Three
Krissa

I sit on a bench overlooking the river. No matter what's going on in my life, the water calms me. Being here shouldn't make me feel so serene, not after all the things that have happened on these banks, but I suppose that's partially why it works. The river reminds me of who I used to be, and how all the events leading up to now make me who I am.

I hear her footsteps before I see her. "I still don't see why we can't just meet at my apartment," Sasha says as she sits down beside me.

It wasn't so long ago that I wanted to claw her eyes out. Literally. She arrived at my house after the Influence spell, after Fox brought me home in the hope that Jodi would know how to help me. The part of my mind that was still me knew she was responsible for what happened and must have alerted the Influence to her status as a possible threat. She was the reason I killed Kai instead of finding some other way out of the situation. It took at least six people to restrain me as Sasha explained to her sister that she'd been able to find a spell to slow down the Influence's inevitable takeover of my body. She was able to enchant my ring—the one that's been passed down from generation to generation in the Barnette line—to keep me tethered to who I am. But with each passing day, the tether is loosening, and we still haven't figured out a way to remove the Influence from my body.

I sigh, tired of repeating my reason for not meeting at her place. "Maybe if your apartment wasn't smack in the center of Main Street. Anyone could see us together there." I shift on the bench, my mind replaying the events that occurred there. "Besides, you know I don't like it there. Too many bad memories."

Sasha snorts. "Don't be so sensitive."

I grit my teeth. It was in that apartment that I began a spell that resulted in the death of a member of my circle. It was in that apartment that I learned Seth—my cousin, the person I had been trusting to help me and my friends—was lying, using me to get what he wanted. But Sasha knows all of this already. "I don't know why you still live there, anyway. The apartment's crap."

Sasha doesn't dignify my comment with a response. Instead, she stands and heads for the river's edge. After a beat, I follow.

"So, any reason you're being extra cloak-and-dagger today?"

There's no point burying the lead. "I just don't want to be overheard. The visions are getting worse. And more frequent. I've had one every day this week. I don't think the spell on the ring will hold much longer."

Sasha touches my arm, making me pause. "None of the visions have come true, right? You're not... You're not using it, are you?"

I shake my head. "No." The corners of my mouth quirk up in a humorless smile. "No magic for me."

"Influence isn't magic," she says quietly.

I nod. I know that better than anyone. Magic comes from nature, and what's inside me is anything but natural. "I don't want to use it. I'm not even tempted. If I'm honest, it's kind of nice being a normal person for once." I close my eyes and exhale. "Except I'm not. Not really. It's always there, beneath the surface. And if what happens in my mind is any indication, it wants out. It *wants* to play out these fantasies for real." I look out at the water again. "I'm scared. I can't help wondering if someday soon the smoke is going to clear and I'll realize it wasn't a vision. I'm terrified I'll actually hurt someone—*kill* someone."

I glance at Sasha and catch an expression as it flickers across her face. I don't have to read her mind to know what she's thinking: *It wouldn't be the first time.*

It's true. I've killed, but only to save the people I care about. Kai shouldn't even count since it was the Influence that made me do it. But since Sasha refrained from coming out and saying it, I won't waste my breath. Sasha's trying to turn over a new leaf, and reopening old wounds won't help either of us. She and I could argue about who's to blame for lots of things, but it won't change our reality now. And although I'm the one with this darkness, this evil swirling inside me, I know Sasha has her own problems. Despite the fact that she helped keep the Influence from taking me over completely, her sister Anya and her best friend Elliot decided she'd crossed a line she can't come back from. Neither will be associated with her anymore.

Sasha's reasons for helping me aren't entirely altruistic. She's desperate to prove she's changed, to prove she's done seeking revenge for Seth's death. But her isolation from the other people in my world is part of why our arrangement works so well for me. She's the only one I can be entirely honest with, because I know everything I tell her will stay between us. She won't worry about me. She won't try to protect me or shield me from myself. She'll work through the problem, and she'll allow me to help—unlike Jodi and Anya, who refuse to even give me status updates about any progress they're making.

A familiar pang shoots through my chest. Sasha is the only one I've told about everything, but she shouldn't be. I should be telling Owen, too, but I don't want him to worry about me any more than he already is. He does his best to hide it, but every once in a while I catch a glimmer of concern on his face when he thinks I'm not paying attention.

"Well, it's a good thing I may have another solution," Sasha says, continuing down the riverbank.

I'm at her side again in an instant. "Really?"

Her mouth works like she's chewing on her words, choosing the best ones to use. "It's a dissevering spell, and it *should* separate the two parts of your personality—you and the Influence. It was designed to suppress negative traits in a person, but I don't see why it wouldn't work in your case."

I do my best to temper my enthusiasm before I've gotten all the details. "So it's like the spell you cast on my ring?"

She shakes her head. "That was designed to tether your mind to your body, to keep the Influence from taking over. But you've always known the Influence was there."

I nod. Even when Sasha and the other witches first cast the spell and my mind was clearer than it is now, I always felt the Influence simmering in the background.

"This spell should separate you from the Influence. It's supposed to build a kind of barrier between you and whatever you don't want controlling your behavior. I doubt it'll hold up indefinitely, but it should buy us enough time to figure out how to get it out of you."

"That sounds perfect."

"Not so fast." She meets my eyes for an instant. "There's a catch."

The bubble that had been swelling in my chest deflates. "Of course there is."

"The spell is supposed to repress a single quality, not a whole entity. If we do it, you could go back to your old self with the Influence locked away, or..."

"Or *I* could get locked away and the Influence could take over."

"Exactly. Like I said, it's designed to deal with particular aspects of your personality, but some people have used it to help with dissociative identity disorder—you know, multiple personalities? From what I've found, when it's used like that, the dominant side always wins out. The weaker one is stuffed down in your subconscious."

If only Sasha had found this spell weeks ago. If she'd located it in the days immediately following the spell, back when the ring was keeping the Influence in check, I wouldn't have hesitated. But now, with the Influence tainting my thoughts daily, I'm not so sure which side would win. What if I'm not stronger than the darkness? I shake my head. "It's too risky."

Not for the first time, I think back to the months after Seth died. I cut myself off from my friends because of what I did. I didn't want to infect them with the evil I thought was inhabiting me.

The thought of it is ridiculous now. I had no idea what true darkness was then. Even the little bits of Influence I'm conscious of are far more frightening than anything that lived inside me before.

"It's your call," Sasha says. "I won't try to convince you to do it if you don't think it'll work."

I offer a tight-lipped smile. I'm sure she could probably persuade me if she tried. She's a master of manipulation. But doing so won't serve either of our best interests. "Actually, I was wondering if you could find a spell that'll keep me from tapping into the Influence at all. I mean, if I can't *use* the Influence, it can't hurt anyone. There's got to be a spell for that, right? For keeping someone from using magic? I mean..." I hold up my wrist and tap the hemp bracelet.

The arc of Sasha's eyebrow tells me what she thinks of my plan—that it's a bandage for a hemorrhaging wound—but she exhales and smiles anyway. "I'll look."

I manage to smile in return. "Thanks."

"Yeah," she says, pivoting on her heel to start back the way we came.

I catch the crook of her arm with mine and tug her until she's facing me. "No. Sasha—thank you."

She holds my gaze for a moment before rolling her eyes. "You're not gonna hug me or something, are you?"

"I'd never dream of offending you like that."

In unison, we start for our cars. Not for the first time, I'm struck by the unlikeliness of our alliance. Before the Influence spell, Sasha was at the top of a short list of people I wouldn't trust under any circumstances; now she's the keeper of my darkest secrets.

My phone vibrates in my back pocket. When I see Owen's name on the screen, I tamp down a wave of guilt. He has no idea I've been talking to Sasha, and if he did, he wouldn't like it. He'd be even more unhappy if he knew why.

Sasha glances at the phone, too. "Date tonight?"

Her tone indicates her opinion on the matter. "Yes, Owen and I are going on a date. Do you have a problem?"

She pulls her keys from her pocket as we approach her dilapidated Honda Civic. "Don't you think you've got more important things to do than playing house with your boyfriend? I'd think with the Influence rearing its ugly head more often you'd want to spend more time alone. Or, you know, maybe spend more time searching for a solution."

"That's not fair—you know Jodi's policing me about doing research." It's not just that Jodi and Anya are close-mouthed about their own progress; they don't want me trying to figure things out on my own. They're afraid I'll try something drastic on my own— which isn't an unfounded fear. Just after the Influence spell, Jodi followed through on a threat to take my phone and limit my access to computers for trying to figure out how to rid myself of the Influence. "I tried pulling away from everyone once. It didn't really help. Besides, being with Owen is one of the few things that keeps me grounded. I don't go red when I'm with him. When we're together, I can almost forget the Influence is inside me at all."

She leans against her car and crosses her arms over her chest, affecting a bad-girl pose. The look is amplified by her unruly dark hair, black tank top, and ripped-knee jeans. All she needs is a chain dangling from her wrist or her pocket. "Maybe forgetting what's going on isn't in your best interest. If you're not thinking about it, you're not fixing it."

"Well, it's a good thing I've got you, then, isn't it?" I offer a wry smile. Sasha opens her mouth to continue, but I cut her off. "I understand where you're coming from. You just need to trust that Owen's not a distraction."

She looks like she wants to argue, but she gives a noisy exhale instead. "I'll text you if I find any info, okay?"

I nod and open the door to my car. Once I'm safely buckled inside, I slide my finger across the screen of my phone to reply to Owen's message. I get where Sasha's coming from, and I'm glad I have her on my side. But my time with Owen isn't just about companionship. I need him. I don't think I could get through this without him.

I hope I'll never have to try.

Chapter Four
Fox

The only spot in the parking lot behind the bookstore is along the back edge. I could roll my truck up and down the aisles a few times in hopes that someone will pull out before the movie starts, but I'm in no mood. The atmosphere in the cab is so tense, I can't wait to feel the balmy air outside.

I feel Dana's eyes on me as I cut the ignition. She's pouting. Again. It seems to be her default setting lately. I take a deep breath before turning to her. I promised we'd spend the evening together and I don't want to give her any reason to be more upset than she already is.

She looks hot, as usual. She's used the warmer weather as an excuse to cover less and less of her body. Tonight, she's in a spaghetti-strap tank top. If it can even be called that. The thing barely covers where her bra would be, if she were wearing one. But she's not—and that fact is tantalizingly obvious through the thin fabric. Her cutoff jeans are so short the pockets hang below the cuffs. And then there are her shoes—high-heeled, gladiator, biker-type things that creep up almost to her knees. Her makeup is impeccable, her hair styled wavy. She'd be completely gorgeous if not for the fact her lower lip is poking out like she's a child.

"What's wrong?" I ask, even though I don't really want to know the answer.

She takes in a deep breath, her chest straining against her tiny shirt. "You've barely said a word since I got into the truck. The whole point of us going out tonight was to spend some quality time together. We barely hang out at all anymore. And when we do, it's like you're somewhere else. Like now."

I sigh. This argument is already getting old. She's been singing the same refrain for weeks now. No matter what I do, I can't seem to make her happy. "I told you. Finals are coming up. My dad's coming down on me hard about applying for colleges."

"I get that," she begins.

"I don't think you do—otherwise you wouldn't keep bringing it up."

Dana shrinks back at the sharpness in my tone and I immediately regret what I've said. I take a second to calm down before continuing.

"Dad says it was always my mom's hope that Griffin and I would have a better life than she did." Mom got pregnant with Griffin when she was in high school, which derailed her plans for higher education. Dad said she wanted to go for a degree once Griffin and I were in school, but destiny had other plans. "Griffin's never going to college, so that leaves me."

Dana softens and guilt twangs my heartstrings. I hate that this is the only card I can play that she'll respond to. Her mom's not a part of her life and her dad died several months back, so she gets the whole dead-parent thing. Sometimes I wonder if it's the only thing we have in common. She reaches forward and covers my hand. "I get that you want to honor your mom." A smile tugs at the corners of her mouth. "It's one of many things I love about you."

The conditioned air in the cab is suddenly oppressive and I struggle to take a breath. Dana leans forward like she's going to kiss me, but I turn and open the door instead. I don't look back as I slam it closed behind me. I wait by the tailgate for her and hold my breath until I catch sight of her face. I luck out, because she looks slightly happier than she did before. Somehow denying her a kiss didn't undo the progress I made in appeasing her.

I probably should've let her kiss me, but it's too late for that now. Instead, I link my hand with hers and lead her to the bookstore's back door. I'm just glad we're not fighting. Tonight will be so much easier to get through if she's not mad at me.

Eyes lock on Dana as soon as we enter the store. After spending the last six months with her, I'm used to it. And I get it: She's hard not to look at. I'm pretty sure I should feel protective or jealous about these guys staring at my girlfriend with thinly veiled lust, but I can't dredge up the emotion.

We have to walk through the main part of the store to get to the concession stand by the Main Street entrance. Once a month, the owner of the bookstore tacks up a white curtain on the store's largest wall and projects a movie based off a book. The quality is crap and the sound is hit-or-miss, but that doesn't keep people from turning out—especially people my age.

There just aren't that many things to do in Clearwater, I guess.

As we stand in line, Dana nuzzles my shoulder. It takes a measure of self-control not to shake her off. I used to be totally into PDAs—especially with her. Call me an asshole, but it's kind of awesome knowing every guy in the vicinity would give a testicle to switch places with you. But lately... Well, mostly I feel guilty about leading her on. I've needed to break up with her for a while, but I have my reasons for staying with her.

But lately I'm wondering if those reasons aren't good enough.

The line shifts and I catch a glimpse of unruly red curls. Lexie Taylor is two people ahead of us in line, fingers entwined with Felix Wolfe's. I'm still not sure how that happened. Lexie is among the most popular girls at school, and Felix... Well, he's not in the same league. He's well-known enough in his own way, I guess, though it's more for his quick wit than anything else. But I suppose things have changed a lot this school year.

As if he picked up on my thoughts, Felix glances back and

catches my eye. He raises his chin in acknowledgment and I do the same. Absently, I rub at the hemp bracelet woven with snowflake obsidian and Apache tears that resides on my left wrist. Of course, Felix didn't *actually* pick up on my thoughts; the bracelet guards against that.

Lexie follows Felix's gaze and smiles when she finds me at the end of it. She waves the people separating us to go ahead of her and Felix in line. "Hey, how's it going? I feel like it's been forever since we talked."

"Oh, ages and ages," I agree, rolling my eyes.

She shoves my shoulder playfully. "You know what I mean. I used to spend almost every free moment in your basement, and now..." She shrugs.

It's true. It was only months ago that the witches used to meet up at my place to practice spells or just hang out—mostly because my dad is usually out of state, driving a truckload of something or other from place to place. It meant I had to live under Griffin's authority, but it also meant we could pretty much do whatever we wanted. But everything is different now. It's been almost two months since the circle met altogether. I assume the others are still practicing magic, but I wouldn't know firsthand.

I nod as the line moves. Felix asks Dana something about a class they share, and while his tone is polite, his smile doesn't quite reach his eyes. I think I know why: If Dana hadn't been so fixated on reclaiming the psychic abilities she lost, Krissa might not have ended up like she is now: filled with Influence that made her explode a dude. But he's polite, which has to mean he's not holding it against her.

The four of us chat until it's our turn to buy popcorn and candy. I'm more than a little glad for the distraction. With any luck, by the time Dana and I snag a seat, the movie will start and I can drape an arm around her to make her feel like the time is quality. I'd rather not get pulled into another conversation about the state of our relationship or—worse—what will happen after we graduate a year from now.

After I pay for the snacks Dana picks out, I find myself behind Lexie and Felix again. They're scanning the seating area for a spot.

"You guys want to join us?" she asks when she notices me.

I open my mouth, ready to say yes and follow their trajectory, but before the word slips out, I notice who they're going to go sit by. Krissa and Owen have claimed a group of folding chairs a few rows back from the sheet. "Nah. Thanks, though," I say, catching Dana's arm as she starts after them. When Dana glances back at me, a confused expression crossing her face, I offer a smile. "Quality time, right? Just the two of us." She smiles, and I know she won't put up a fight. After a quick look around, I notice a pair of seats in the back row on the other side of the space. "How about right there?"

Dana nods before starting for the chairs. I'm about to follow when something grazes my elbow. Felix leans in when I turn back. "You gotta get over it eventually, man."

Before I can even open my mouth, he's off after Lexie, who's already halfway to the seats Krissa and Owen saved for them.

Irritation builds as I edge between rows to join Dana. Get over it? What the hell does he know about it? Oh, I forgot—*everything*, apparently. After Krissa and Crystal went back in time and found themselves here, but without the benefit of the memories of their lives in this reality, Felix was the person Krissa opened up to. He knew weeks before I did that the girl I'd been dating for years no longer existed for all intents and purposes. It pisses me off that he thinks that fact gives him the right to talk to me like he knows something. He doesn't know *anything*.

When I reach Dana, I shove the cup caddy and snacks at her. Surprise flicks across her face and I have to wonder what expression is contorting mine. "I'm getting popcorn."

She settles the cups down on the seat beside her and holds up the brown paper bag filled with candy. "But... we never get popcorn."

"Well, I want some tonight," I snap.

Hurt flashes in her eyes. "I'm sorry. I should've let you pick the snacks tonight. I can go get it if you want."

I shake my head before turning and stepping over feet and between legs to get back to the concession table. I was a dick to her just then—more like my brother than myself. I should've apologized, but I need a minute. Why does everything have to be so jacked up right now?

The line of last-minute snack-buyers is longer than the one I stood in before. As I wait, my gaze isn't drawn to Dana, but to Krissa. Her pale blonde hair is pulled back into a messy bun atop her head, probably to keep it from sticking to her neck. When we were together, she was forever complaining about how warm she got in the summer. I always suggested she wear her hair like it is now, but she would never do it—I doubt Crystal Jamison would've approved. It doesn't fit the polished aesthetic she, Lexie, and Bridget Burke always went for, so Krissa couldn't do it either. Of course, this version of Krissa never cared about such things. She tips her head back and laughs at something Felix is saying, and Owen slips his arm around her shoulders. I should look away, but I can't, not even when she and Owen kiss.

It's torture, but I'm incapable of fighting it.

The bookstore's main lights dim and a chorus of cheers shoots up. An employee turns on the projector and the buzz of conversation dials back a few levels, although it doesn't die down completely. Krissa stands, and after planting another kiss on her boyfriend's mouth, she slips out of the aisle and disappears behind the nearest bookcase. I squint, attempting to follow her progress. There's nothing in that direction but the bathrooms.

There's only a flicker of hesitation in my step as I leave the line and follow her. The projector is finally warmed up and the opening frames of tonight's movie are filling the sheet, so everyone's attention is at the front of the room. No one notices as I head toward the bathrooms.

Krissa's hand is almost on the door to the ladies' room when she pauses. When she turns, she gives a little start. "Fox, what are you...?" She allows the sentence to fall off. Her eyes close and she gives herself a little shake before opening them again. When her gaze fixes on me, her brown eyes are brighter, full of a mischievous gleam I've seen more times than I can count—any time we snuck kisses in class while the teacher's head was turned, or when she'd brush up close against me in my basement while the circle was focusing on a spell.

In three steps, she's crossed to me. Her arms snake around me, her hands finding the nape of my neck. I dip my face down and she tilts hers up so our lips meet. She presses in and kisses me so hard she nearly takes my breath away.

We're taking a risk—a bigger one than usual—but with Krissa pressed up against me like this, I can't think clearly. Someone could see us—Owen or Dana might come looking for one of us—but I don't care.

Felix told me I need to get over it, but he doesn't understand. There's nothing to get over. Soon everyone else will know it, too.

Chapter Five
Brody

The repository is one of the most beautiful buildings in town—not that anyone but an Amaranthine would ever know it.

My people have lived here for generations, almost since the split with the Devoted soon after Seth was locked away in a quartz crystal. Like Clearwater, this place, hemmed in on all sides by an ancient forest, is full of magic. There are certain places in the world where the pulse of magic is stronger, and people with abilities are irresistibly drawn to them. Unlike Clearwater, however, this refuge in southern Illinois has been spelled by powerful witches to appear ruined and empty, and to make anyone without abilities feel unsettled when they draw near.

But that's not the history I'm interested in today. I push open the heavy wooden doors and enter the repository. As always, I'm in awe of the beauty of the space. The vaulted ceilings and natural light give it a warm feeling, despite the fact the air is always cool. I'm not here to appreciate the architecture, though, or enjoy the heady, musty smell. Today, I have only one thing in mind: learning as much as possible about Influence.

I've heard of it, of course. Its power turns up like the bogeyman in scary stories told by children and in morality tales shared by adults. But fact often blends with fiction, and I need to separate the two if I want to be successful in my endeavor.

I promised Jade an assassin whose power and ruthlessness

would be unmatched by any who try to stand against her. But I'm not entirely sure I can keep that promise.

There are a dozen people milling around different areas of the repository. I'm sure at least one of them works here, but I'm not in the mood to ask for assistance. I don't know my way around here nearly as well as I ought to, but I know enough to get started. Like any library, the texts here are divided by subject, and dark occult practices are located in the east wing. I take care to stroll at a leisurely pace as I make my way there. One drawback of being in the running to become the next high priest is that everyone knows my face. Occasionally, people will stop me to chat—usually to request that I do something for them. Typically I'm able to smile and nod through such distractions, but I don't have time for pleasantries today. I don't want to give Jade an excuse to seek help from anyone else—especially not Lena Wiley.

There is danger in bringing someone from outside into our ranks. Kai was loyal to us because we had years to build his trust, to direct his rage. After the events that led to Krissa's current condition, she has no reason to pledge her allegiance to us. There is the promise of power, of course—but she already possesses the strongest power I've ever heard of. She doesn't need us for that. Luckily I can give her something else: a target for her rage. The Amaranthine always have a target in need of punishment.

What if it's still not enough? I trail my finger over a nearby shelf. My nose wrinkles automatically at the collection of dust that gathers there. The east wing isn't a place frequented by many.

Perhaps there's a way to bind her allegiance to us. It's worth looking into. If such a spell exists, it would surely be found here. I murmur an incantation, a simple locater spell to point me in the right direction. As my fingertips brush the spine of a black book with gold lettering, movement in the corner of my eye catches my attention.

I drop my hand as I turn. Lena Wiley stands in the doorway,

head cocked curiously to the side. I bite back a curse. Of course she works here. She's a researcher. I should've been more on guard as I walked through.

"Can I help you?" I ask, even though she should probably be the one to ask the question.

She doesn't respond right away. Her eyes flick to the shelf behind me and I'm positive she's trying to figure out which book I was reaching for. "Do you really think it'll work?" she asks, taking a step into the room.

I lift an eyebrow. She's talking like we're continuing a conversation. While I'm certain I know what's she's asking, I refuse to engage her so informally. If she wants to know something, she can be specific.

After a long pause, a smile curves her lips. She seems to sense what I'm thinking, even though I'm fairly certain she's not a psychic. There aren't many psychics in the Amaranthine. Most of those who split off from the Devoted were witches, and it's magic that thrives in our blood. The few psychics in our community hold jobs related to advising and information gathering. If she had those abilities, she wouldn't be a research assistant.

"You've got a reputation, you know that?" she asks, curling her fingers over the back of a chair and leaning forward.

She's still being indirect. Two can play at this. "Do I, now?" Too bad I can't get a read on her. I'm usually good at judging people, but she's tricky.

"The women think you're charming. Is that your plan with Krissa Barnette? Are you going to charm her into being the assassin?"

I grit my teeth. So that's her angle—she's on a fact-finding mission. Her reputation plus her impertinence when it comes to proper decorum with Jade is helping me paint a picture of her ambitions. She's after the same thing I am. Does this child honestly think she has a chance at becoming the next high priestess? The idea is so absurd it's almost laughable.

But for some reason, I can't bring myself to laugh. Something tugs at the back of my mind. What if I can't convince Krissa to take the position? If Jade counts that as another failing, what does that do to my chances of taking her place when she steps down? And what if it's Lena who impresses her in the meantime? While the Amaranthine vote, the exiting priestess's nod is nearly a guarantee of victory.

When I don't respond, Lena pushes away from the chair. As she strides toward me, her eyes don't leave my face. "You know, I always thought Kai was the absolute perfect specimen of an assassin. His magical prowess paired with his bloodlust..." She shakes her head, that same smile playing about the corners of her lips. "There was talk in some circles about how he'd die of old age before anyone managed to beat him for the job. But now, because of you, it seems there *is* someone better. I have to admit, there's no one on any list I could come up with who sounds as qualified as this Barnette girl. She killed Seth. She killed Kai. Who could beat that?"

She's an arm's length away now. Her words are carefully chosen to flatter me, but her trick won't work: I've done this to too many people in my day to be taken in by it—especially when the tactic is performed by an amateur. My posture relaxes. I can't believe I felt threatened by her for even a moment.

"I could help you," she continues, sliding closer. She's a full head shorter than I am and she peers up at me through her long eyelashes. "I pretty much know everything there is to know—and what I'm not sure of, I can find faster than you can blink. I'd be an asset in Clearwater, don't you think?"

The laugh I couldn't muster before bubbles up my throat and over my lips. Lena takes a hasty step back, her green eyes flashing. "No, Lena," I say through my chuckles. "I neither want nor need your help."

The lines of her face harden. The transformation is so quick it's almost amazing. In less than a second, she switches from an innocent girl to an angry woman. "You don't want to make me your enemy, Brody."

I tilt my head and study her. "That sounds like a threat."

"Take it however you want," she says, her voice low. "But remember that you're about to leave Jade's side for who knows how long. And I'm going to be right here. Be sure you don't screw up in Clearwater. Again." Her smile returns. "On second thought—go ahead."

She blows a kiss and pivots before I can respond. I have half a mind to follow her, but what would I say? What *can* I say? If I threaten her back, it's because I see her as an equal, and I don't want her to think that for a second.

My superior feelings from moments ago have evaporated. What she's saying is true. When I'm not here, she'll be the voice in Jade's ear. How long before Jade starts looking at her in that special way again? How long before I slip from the favored spot I hold? Jade already thinks I've failed. I've got no room for error on this mission. I have to convince Krissa to become our assassin, and the sooner the better. It's barely a month before Jade's twenty-five-year term comes to an end. So little time, but also so much. What kind of damage could someone like Lena do in that amount of time?

Chapter Six
Krissa

The house is quiet—or as quiet as the three-story Victorian place ever is. There are the usual groans and sighs to be expected from a house this old, but for the moment, there are no voices.

I wish I could luxuriate in a quiet Saturday all to myself, but I have work to do. After pouring myself a mug of tea, I make my way into the living room and collapse onto the couch. The coffee table is littered with mailings from every college under the sun. I'll be a senior next year, which apparently means universities all over the country suddenly find me very interesting.

If they only knew.

No matter how many hints I sneak into conversations with my parents, I can't convince them that maybe college isn't the path for me. They think the Influence is in check—and I want them to believe that. I want them to believe I'm wholly their daughter, unhindered by any crazy, magic-related fate.

Even Owen's been talking about applications. When he starts going on and on about essays and transcripts, I can almost pretend life really is that simple.

For him, I suppose it is.

I scan the names on the envelopes as I sip my tea, trying to remember which schools Owen said he's applying to. Maybe I'll apply to the same places and follow him to whichever school he chooses. If someone else were to tell me that was her plan for selecting a school, I'd probably throw up a little. But I'm not in the same situation as most people. I can't imagine not being able to see Owen every day. I wasn't lying when I told Sasha he's the only thing that keeps me centered. If we're not able to get the Influence out of me, I'm afraid to think what might happen if we're separated by more than a couple of miles.

I shake my head. College is still more than a year away. There's no reason to think we won't be able to come up with a permanent solution by then.

I'll keep telling myself that, anyway.

I select a few envelopes based solely on their logos and fonts. After tearing open a few and scanning the contents, I'm no closer to narrowing down the pile than I was before. Everything sounds so generic: beautiful campus, accredited programs, close-knit community.

Felix and Lexie are also going through this process. They talked about it a little at the movie last night. From what I overheard, it doesn't sound like either of them will be making their ultimate decision based on the other. I wonder how Fox and Dana are going to handle the college thing. Are they even planning on going? Fox is smart enough—or at least he puts in enough effort to do the spells to get good grades. But Griffin didn't go, so maybe he'll follow in his brother's footsteps. And Dana barely makes enough effort to get to school on time on a regular basis. I can't see higher education as a top priority for her.

A knock sounds on the front door, pulling me from my thoughts. I stiffen, listening for clues as to who might be on the porch. A couple weeks ago, a pair of people carrying religious tracts showed up. They talked with Jodi for nearly half an hour before Dad got home and convinced them to move on. But there's no sound now, not like there would be if two people were chatting while waiting for the door to open.

Another knock. I breathe out a curse as I stand. A lot of the time, not being a psychic anymore doesn't faze me: After all, I spent months blocking off the part of my abilities that would enable me to figure out who was nearby. But then there are other times, like now, when the absence is so sharp it sends a pang through my chest.

I steel myself and open the door, prepared to tell the visitor I'm underage and therefore can't buy whatever he might be selling, but I stop short when I look through the screen door. It's Crystal.

"Hey," she says, offering a smile that dissipates too quickly. "Can I come in?"

It takes me a moment to find my voice. It's not like this is the first time Crystal's been to my house. It's just she never comes unannounced or without a reason, so I'm automatically on alert. "Sure."

She pulls open the screen door, but I don't wait until she enters before retracing my steps to the living room. I don't know that we've been alone together since the night of the Influence spell. We've talked, of course. We still sit together at school; our interactions are pleasant. I've done my best to make my peace with what happened that night. It was my choice to sacrifice my abilities so the Influence would fill me, and not her and Dana. Still, a pulse of energy crackles just beneath my skin when I think about how she's only a witch again because she's using my magic.

Crystal joins me on the couch, and before I can ask why she's here, she's talking. "Are you okay?"

I search her face. Where is this coming from? In the days immediately following the spell, I heard that question about a billion times from all my well-meaning friends, but since then, everyone seems to have assumed I'm adjusting, that the ring spell is holding. Has she been talking to Sasha? The crackle in my veins builds and I take a breath to bring it back down to a simmer. Of course that's not the case. In addition to the fact that I can't imagine Crystal talking to Sasha under any circumstances, I also trust that Sasha wouldn't share what I've told her in confidence. "I'm fine."

She shakes her head like she was expecting that answer. "I don't think you are. I'm worried about you."

I cross my arms over my chest. "Please. I don't need anyone else worrying about me. You should see Jodi and Anya." The two have spent every bit of their free time in the last two months trying to figure out how to undo the Influence spell. When they're around me, they're always poking and prodding, asking me questions and trying to force teas and tinctures down my throat. If there's such a thing as being cared-for to death, I'm in danger of it. Jodi's even stepped down as manager of her homeopathic shop in town to devote more time to research. "I'm not sure why you care so much, anyway."

Hurt flashes in Crystal's eyes. "Of course I care—you're my friend. I know we don't talk about it, but don't think a day goes by that I'm not thankful for what you did for me. I just want to make sure—"

"What? That I don't go Dark Side?" I know she's trying to be helpful, but I can't help the flare of irritation—of anger—that surges inside me. "You have no idea what I'm going through."

"I know." There's a beat before she continues, and when she does, her voice is quiet. "You pulled away after what happened with Seth, and I don't want you to go down that road again. You can tell me anything. I'll understand."

"Really? Anything?" I stand, the sizzling in my veins making it impossible to sit still. "Can I tell you about how I keep fantasizing about ripping people's heads off? About making them explode the way Kai did? How part of me isn't horrified by those ideas?" I shouldn't be telling her any of this. I've worked hard to keep these things inside. But the look of horror spreading across her face gives me a sick sense of satisfaction. "Don't pretend like you want to know what's going on in my head. It's your fault I'm like this—if you would've listened to me in the first place about Influence, this never would've happened."

Crystal is on her feet now, too. The terror of a moment ago has evaporated, replaced by a kind of indignation that suits her much better. "What do you want me to say? I'm sorry—is that it? I've said it I don't know how many times."

"Oh, yes," I growl sarcastically. "That makes it all better." Why is she even here? She says she's worried about me. Well, she should be, but there's nothing she can do to help. "Let's be honest: you don't really care about me, you're just here because you feel guilty."

She shakes her head. "You know me better than that. I saw something in your eyes in history yesterday. Now I guess I know what." Her stone-blue eyes study my face. "Does Jodi know about these fantasies you're having? Or are you still keeping secrets from everyone?"

I don't like the way she's talking, the way she's looking at me. "You can't tell her."

She throws her hands up. "I can't believe you're keeping this from her. She thinks everything's okay—we all do. You can't lie to us, not about this."

"Why? Why should I tell everyone the truth? So they can all look at me the way you are right now?"

"No, so we can help you." In a flash, her cell phone is in her hand.

My fingers itch with the desire to rip it away. My tingling skin reminds me I could use the Influence to take it from her. "What are you doing?" I ask, trying my best to keep my voice even.

"I'm calling Jodi," she says. "She needs to know."

"You can't do that." I lunge for her phone, but she twists her body and holds her hand out so I can't reach it. The screen display indicates she's already opened her contact list, and her thumb scrolls through the alphabet toward the J's. "Crystal, I'm begging you. Don't call her."

She glances at me over her shoulder. "The fact that you don't want me to makes me think this is the right thing to do."

I have to stop her. I can't let her call Jodi. Sasha knows the truth about how the Influence is affecting me, and that's enough. I don't need to burden my aunt any more. She's already lost too much because of me. I try to push past Crystal, to reach for her outstretched hand, but in a flash she elbows me backward and holds me in place with a spell. I can still move my arms and legs, but I can make no forward progress. It's as if an invisible barrier has been erected between us.

She's using magic on me. She's using *my* magic *against* me.

When the red creeps into my periphery, it's not in the slow, subtle way it usually comes. It unfurls and clouds my vision until all I can see is Crystal's face. She has to stop. I have to make her stop.

My skin is burning. I lift my hand and hold it out toward Crystal. When I curl my fingers, she reaches for her neck. Her phone slips from her hand and she sputters, trying to draw in a breath.

Why wouldn't she just listen to me? Why wouldn't she just do what I asked? This is her fault. She asked for this.

I raise my arm and Crystal's feet leave the floor. She kicks them as if doing so will help her in some way. Her hands continue to claw at her throat, but there's nothing to pull away. As her eyes bulge, the heat in my body begins to crescendo. The world is burning—it must be, because I'm on fire. If I release Crystal, if I stop drawing on the Influence, the pain will end.

But I don't stop.

Crystal's feet jerk rather than kick, and her head lolls to the side. It's almost over now.

The solid *thunk* of car doors slamming reaches me. A quick glance out the window reveals my parents. They're on their way in.

I blink.

The full weight of the situation crashes down on me as the red drains from my vision. I drop my arm and Crystal crumples to the floor. My parents can't find her like this. I need more time.

There's another swell of heat, and when I glance out the window again, my parents are frozen in mid-step. I have no idea what I just did or how long it will last, but at least it'll buy me a few moments.

I rush to Crystal's side. I press my fingers to her neck to check for a pulse, but as I do, she rouses. When her eyes land on me, she skitters backward on the floor like a crab.

"Get away from me!"

I reach for her. "It's okay. It's me; it's me."

But the words don't calm her. If it's even possible, they make her panic more. "You just tried to kill me! Help! Help! Somebody!"

I dart forward fast enough to catch her off guard and clamp my hand over her mouth. A ripple like electricity caresses my skin. "Be quiet."

Crystal's mouth opens and closes, but no sound comes out. I glance out the window. My parents are still frozen. When I turn back to Crystal, I know exactly what to do.

"You're not going to remember this. Any of this." The sizzling in my veins reaches every inch of my body. Crystal's eyes slide gently out of focus. "You're going to get up, you're going to leave this house, and you're going to go for a long walk before heading home. That's why you left the house in the first place, to take a walk."

Crystal's head bobs like one of those dashboard dogs. "A walk," she repeats.

I nod. "Yes. You went for a walk. You're not worried about me. You're impressed by how I'm handling myself with all that's going on." I stand, and when I offer her my hand, she doesn't flinch. I pull her to her feet, and without being prompted, she walks robotically toward the door. I follow behind, watching as she takes measured steps down the street. When she turns the corner, my parents are back in motion.

Before they can see me, I close the door and dart up the stairs. As I ascend to the second floor and then the third, my irritation grows. But it's not until I make it to my room that I recognize the source: I'm not mad at Crystal for trying to call Jodi, and I'm not mad at myself for what I almost did to stop her. I'm mad at my parents because they came home and interrupted me.

I cross to my bed and sink onto the mattress. What's wrong with me? Am I so desperate to keep my secret that I'm willing to kill a friend?

Jodi and Anya are working to find a way to get the Influence out of me, but what if they're too late? I need to get this under control before I seriously hurt someone. Next time there might not be an interruption.

Chapter Seven
Fox

I hiss and pull my hand away from the still-hot pasta shells. The steam rising off them should have been warning enough, but I'm on the clock and I want dinner to be ready before she gets here. It's a good thing the stuffed shells need to cook for at least half an hour—it'll give me plenty of time to clean up the kitchen.

I can't believe what a disaster it is in here. This is why I don't usually take the time to cook things from scratch. There's no need most of the time, especially since I'm usually the only one in the house these days. And if I'm honest, she and I have been together long enough for her to know this isn't my forte. But that's also part of why I want to do it. I want to surprise her, to impress her. She deserves it.

I tried cooking for her only once before, and it was a complete disaster. I made chicken Parmesan, and even though the outside of the meat burned, the inside was still pink and raw when I cut into it.

I probably shouldn't have been so ambitious with this dish, but I guess I'm an optimist. Besides, she's always loved Italian food.

When I try opening the shell again, it's cool enough that I don't burn my fingertips. I scoop a spoonful of the ricotta filling and scrape it off inside. That wasn't so hard. Maybe I can manage this after all.

I've just slipped the pan into the oven when I hear the front door open. A smile tugs at the corners of my mouth. She's early. She'll see the mess, which isn't ideal, but it's good to know she was in a rush to get here. I set the timer before heading toward the living room to greet her. "Just can't wait to see me, huh?"

I freeze halfway through the dining room. Griffin stands in the living room, a full garbage bag dangling from his hand.

"What the hell are you doing here?"

"Good to see you too, little brother." He raises an eyebrow.

I attempt to smile, but the muscles in my face are stiff. "Seriously. You never visit. What's up?" Griffin has barely stepped foot in this house since he moved out just after New Year's. What on earth could be bringing him here now?

"What's up? You ever think maybe I just came to chat?"

I stare at him. He has to be joking. We're not exactly a touchy-feely kind of family, and I don't think I've ever heard him use the word *chat* before. Chatting is something girls do at sleepovers, which means it's not something Griffin would ever touch with a ten-foot pole. Does he know I have a date? Is that why he's here? But if that's the case, why isn't he saying anything about it?

The innocent look on Griffin's face cracks and he grins. "The laundromat had a power outage," he says, raising the bag in his hand. "I really need some clean clothes. Figured I could kill some time here while my stuff is washing. I haven't kicked your ass at Military Smackdown in ages." As he talks, he pushes past me on his way toward the basement stairs, but when he gets to the kitchen, he stops in his tracks. "Trying to impress someone?"

"No. Just making dinner." I try to keep my voice casual. "Who would I be trying to impress?"

Griffin gives me a look I've seen about a million times before— the one that says I'm an idiot. "Your girlfriend, I assume. Is Dana gonna be here soon?"

The tense knot that's been forming in my chest for the last few minutes starts to loosen. I hold up my hands innocently. "You got me. She'll be here soon. We had a fight, and I'm trying to make it up to her."

Griffin waggles his eyebrows. "You gonna make things up to her so she'll have a reason to make them up to you?" He throws a few fake punches at my stomach before cupping me on the shoulder and giving a congratulatory shake. "Fine, I'll leave. Just let me get my stuff started. I'll even make you a deal—if you promise to stick my clothes in the dryer later, I won't come back until tomorrow morning before work." He nudges me in the ribs conspiratorially.

"Yeah, yeah. Of course, man. You got it." I'll agree to anything to get him out of here. A glance at the clock on the microwave tells me it's almost time for her to show up. Was that a car door slamming? She usually doesn't drive, but what if she did this time? Is she already here? Griffin can't be here when she comes in. "Tell you what—I'll even get it started for you."

That last bit may have been too much. Griffin squints as he studies me. "Let me guess, she's going to be here any minute?"

I nod, but I'm not sure if it's the right thing to do. Is he suspicious?

He stares for a beat longer. "I know what's going on."

My mind spins. I knew it'd come out eventually, but I never imagined it'd be like this—that Griffin would be the first to find out. What am I going to tell him? How am I going to explain?

But he's grinning again. "You're afraid when she gets here she'll finally ask herself why she's with my dorky little brother when she could be with a real man like me."

A relieved sigh escapes my lips. "Yeah, you wish." I try to keep my tone light, but I'm not sure I'm quite hitting the mark. "But if it makes you feel better, sure. Get out before she sees you and decides to go home with you instead of staying here with me."

Griffin allows me to push him toward the front door. "Okay, I'm going. But make sure you actually do my laundry; otherwise, next time I see her, the naked baby pictures are coming out."

"Yeah, yeah. I'll consider myself warned."

Griffin crosses the threshold, but before stepping off the porch, he spins on his heel to land one soft punch in my gut. Before I can retaliate, he jumps off the porch and jogs to his Mustang. After he's inside he takes a moment to check himself in the rearview mirror, and I fist my hands, digging my nails into my palms. She's going to be here any second. He needs to leave *now*.

I scan the street as Griffin pulls out of the driveway. His car is barely out of sight when she turns onto the road from the opposite direction. She's riding her bike, as usual, and her pale blonde hair streams out behind her like a banner. She catches my eye and smiles as she pedals up the driveway. I close the front door and jog through the house to open the side one. She's just reached it when I push it open.

"Was that Griffin's car I saw?" Krissa asks.

I stretch my arm across the doorway, planting my hand on the opposite jamb to block her entrance. "Maybe."

She glances up at me. "What? I can't come in?"

I can't help smiling. She's so beautiful. "Gotta pay the toll."

She bites her lower lip before tilting her head up. I bend down and press a kiss to her lips. She pulls away quickly and darts under my arm, giggling as she climbs the short flight into the kitchen. But once she enters, she comes to a complete stop. "You cooked?"

I shut the door before joining her. I step in close behind her and wrap my arms around her waist. "Yeah. I told you to come hungry, didn't I?"

She spins inside the circle of my arms to face me. "Well, yeah, but I figured you were going to order pizza."

I grin. "You impressed?"

"Oh, yes," she says, smiling mischievously.

I lean down to kiss her again, and when our lips meet, she takes a step backward, pulling me with her. But with her second step, she stumbles over the bag Griffin dropped on the floor.

"What's this?"

"Griffin's laundry. I guess there was a power outage at the laundromat, but he promised not to come back until tomorrow if I do it for him."

That familiar glint of mischief shines in Krissa's eye. "Good. That means we have plenty of time to ourselves." Her hands find the back of my neck and she pulls me in close for another kiss. I wrap my arms more tightly around her body. She feels so good pressed against me like this. I've missed her so much.

I wish we didn't have to keep this a secret. I wish I could've just told Griffin she was coming over. I don't like lying, but when she's kissing me like this, all those worries melt away. I look forward to the day when we can tell everyone the truth.

Chapter Eight
Krissa

"Krissa, we're ready for you," Jodi calls from the hallway.

Owen tugs on our linked hands. "I guess everyone's here."

I don't budge from my spot on the sofa in the sitting room. Last night when Jodi informed me she and Anya were calling a meeting to discuss the Influence, I was almost relieved. A meeting means they think they've found something that might help. But the more I've been thinking about it, the more unsettled I've become.

I don't talk Influence with my friends. After the first few days post-spell—when it became clear I wasn't going to start indiscriminately murdering anyone who annoyed me—the elephant in the room seemed to blend in with its surroundings. Having them here now will only remind them of how messed up I really am, and I don't want that. I can't stand the idea of my closest friends constantly giving me side-eye as they wait for me to snap.

I chose the spot strategically. It's the last room before the greenhouse, and by sitting here, I ensured I wouldn't be seen as each person entered the house. I'm afraid of what I might see in their eyes, and the meeting hasn't even started yet. "I shouldn't have let Jodi invite so many people."

Owen sighs and rubs the back of my hand with his thumb. "They all care about you. They want to help."

I know he's right, but that doesn't mean I have to like it. I want everyone to believe I'm doing okay. This year has been crazy for all of us and I don't want to be the one causing more stress. I want them to see me as strong—not like a bomb ready to go off.

Even though Dad and Jodi haven't come out and said it, any Influence talk is off-limits around my mom. I can still see the look on her face when Jodi first explained to her what happened. She does her best to put it out of her mind, but there's a nervous look in her eyes sometimes when she thinks I'm not watching. I don't want everyone else to have to hide that same look.

Maybe they already do.

Owen tugs at my hand again, and I can't think of a reason to stay seated. Besides, Jodi will come and get me if I wait much longer.

A buzz of voices carries down the hall from the dining room. Most of the chairs are already filled. Lexie and Felix sit beside each other. Every few seconds one of them touches the other. It's casual—fingers trailing down an arm or brushing a strand of hair off a cheek. I'm glad they're happy. With so much craziness going on in my world, it's good to know some simple pleasures still exist.

Across from Lexie and Felix are Griffin and Tucker Ingram. Although the three of us are not as close as we were in the early months of this year, their friendship hasn't wavered. They were there for me when I needed them most, and I'll never forget them for that. I'm not surprised they're here now. They've proven time and again how much they care for me.

Jodi sits at the head of the table and Anya sits to her right. Owen and I take the only free seats. Eyes flick to me as I settle into the chair opposite my aunt, but the gazes are all friendly—eager, even.

Jodi clears her throat to call attention to herself. Any remnants of conversation die down as all eyes fix on her. "As I'm sure you know, Anya and I have been trying to find a way to get the Influence out of Krissa. It pretty much boils down to this: once it's inside someone, it's a real bitch to get out."

Nervous laughter circles the table. I'm the only one who doesn't smile—besides Anya and Jodi. I appreciate my aunt trying to lighten the mood, but this is serious, and getting more so by the day.

Jodi continues. "As you can imagine, there's not a lot of detail about this spell out there—at least not much that we've been able to find. What we've been able to piece together suggests Influence only releases its grip on a person when she dies."

A fist of dread tightens around my stomach. That's it, then. This evil is going to reside in me for the rest of my life.

A grin cracks Griffin's face. "Okay, then. That's easy: we kill Krissa."

Felix bangs his hand on the table. "That's not funny, Griffin. Stop being such a dick, will you?"

Griffin's demeanor darkens in an instant, his eyes going stormy the way his brother's often do. "Learn to take a joke. Why are you even here, psychic? When we do find a spell, how exactly can you help?"

Felix presses his hands into the table like he means to stand. Lexie brushes his arm with her fingertips, but the motion does little to calm him. Energy starts to spark under my skin. "I'm here to help. Play the witch card all you want, but you know damn well I've got power to contribute to any spell you can throw at me."

Griffin snorts. "Come at me, psychic. I dare you."

The muscles in Felix's arms tense. "Yeah, keep talking."

Electricity thrums and ripples under my skin. The Influence thrives off their discord; it wants to join in, to add to the chaos. I need them to stop arguing, but I also don't want them to.

Griffin opens his mouth, but before he can get the words out, Jodi holds up her hand. "While this is very entertaining, we have more important things to deal with right now. If you two boys can zip your pants back up, I'd like to let you know why we're here."

Lexie doesn't quite hide a snort of laughter. Felix shoots her a wounded look, but she just shrugs.

Owen shifts beside me. "Are you saying you found a way to get the Influence out of Krissa?"

Jodi and Anya exchange glances. Jodi inclines her head, and Anya is the one to answer the question. "The more I've been thinking, the more I wonder if Influence isn't a lot like an invading spirit. It's possible we can get it out of Krissa with an exorcism spell."

I sit up straighter. "Okay, let's do it. We have all the things, don't we? And it's not like this would be the first one you guys performed."

Jodi presses her lips together. "It's not that easy."

"Of course it's not," Tucker grumbles. "Why would anything be that easy?"

Jodi offers a small smile. "If this works, when the Influence leaves Krissa, it'll be looking for a new home."

"So what's the problem?" Lexie asks. "All of us have abilities. I thought the Influence would only take over someone without them. I mean, that's why Krissa..."

Anya and Jodi are both nodding.

"Now that the Influence is in our plane, it's possible it can travel farther to find a new host," Anya says. "Influence isn't something that's going to give up without a fight. The fact is, we aren't dealing with a spirit. That means we have to move forward with every precaution."

"Let me guess," Griffin says, leaning back in his chair, "we're gonna wait till the full moon."

Jodi touches her nose with her pointer finger. "Bingo. With the power of the moon behind us, we should be able to keep the Influence from any funny business."

"Should," Felix mutters.

Lexie slaps him on the arm. He holds up his hands innocently and she purses her lips. "What if... What if it doesn't work?" she asks.

There's a flicker of hesitation as Anya and Jodi exchange glances again. "If it doesn't work, we'll have to try something else," Jodi says. To her credit, she makes it sound like it wouldn't be that big of a deal, like we have dozens of other options to choose from. But despite the fact that I'm no longer psychic, I know what she's thinking: if this doesn't work, they don't have a plan B.

I could mention the dissevering spell Sasha told me about, but something stops me. It's not that I don't want them to know I've been in contact with Sasha—to the contrary, I've been trying to convince her to let me tell Anya and Elliot for weeks now. Instead, the fear prickling in the back of my mind is that they'll want to try the spell, and I'm not sure I'm strong enough to be the one who wins out.

But there's really no need to tell them—not right now. There's every likelihood the exorcism will work.

Jodi goes over some plans for how we'll meet up on the day of the full moon. I tune her out. My attention comes back to the room when chairs begin scraping against the wood floors as people stand to leave. Jodi and Anya excuse themselves to the greenhouse, ostensibly to make preparations, but probably to do more research to formulate a backup plan. Lexie, Felix, Griffin, and Tucker all say their goodbyes. I walk them to the door, and to Owen's credit, he doesn't even flinch when Tucker surprises me with a farewell hug.

When I start for the living room, Owen follows, linking his hand with mine. "Don't worry about anything," he says as we settle on the couch. "This is going to work." He brushes the fingers of his free hand against my cheek, persuading me to turn my face and meet his eyes. "You believe me, right?"

I force a smile and nod. It's the reaction he expects. "Of course."

He leans forward to kiss me, and I try to lose myself in the sensation. Usually being close to Owen makes all my doubts and fears disappear, but it's not working today. I do my best to push down the swell of doubt rising within me. I was there for Crystal's exorcism spell. Bess Taylor fought hard when we attempted to remove her spirit from Crystal's body. How much harder will the Influence fight? And it's not as if the exorcism was without lasting consequences for Crystal. Although she was a natural-born witch, when she awoke after the spell, all of her magic was gone. I'm already without any powers, except those granted by the Influence. What more could it take from me once it's cast out?

Owen cradles my face as he deepens our kiss and I press myself close to him. I can't dwell on all the what-ifs. I have to believe it will work and everything will be fine. Otherwise, what am I even fighting for?

Chapter Nine
Brody

I finish drawing the circle on the ground and slip the piece of chalk back into its plastic bag before pocketing it. My nose wrinkles as I study the fingers of my right hand. White dust stands out against my skin, but with a wave of my left hand, it disappears, leaving my flesh looking as perfect as ever.

I've only just arrived in Clearwater, but there's no sense in dragging things out. I need to talk to Krissa, and now is as good a time as ever.

From my back pocket, I remove a brown paper bag. I pull out a piece of smoky quartz similar to the one set in the ring Krissa always wears, along with a picture of Owen Marsh that I snapped while doing surveillance the last time I was in town. I set the two items in the center of the circle, but it will take three to draw her here. When I was considering elements to place within the summoning circle, the first two came easily. The third was a little trickier. But when I finally struck on it, I couldn't believe it took me so long.

I murmur an incantation and draw a line across my right palm with my left pointer finger. As if I had sliced it with the blade, the skin opens and bleeds. I fist my hand and hold it over the center of the circle until three drops fall. Another incantation and the wound knits itself closed. If I were simply seeking Krissa, the blood would not draw her here, but I'm not just summoning her—I'm summoning the Influence within her.

All I have to do now is wait. I stroll back to my car and take a seat behind the steering wheel. No one can resist the irresistible tug of a summoning circle, not unless there has been some serious spellwork to hide them specifically from such magic. But there's no reason to believe Krissa has done that. I drum my fingers on the steering wheel as the minutes tick by.

Within a quarter of an hour, my patience is rewarded. I chose this particular stretch of road with care. Clearwater is far from a bustling metropolis, but there are few roads that get little to no traffic. This is one of them. When the car comes into view, I know it must be hers before it's close enough for me to tell.

When she emerges from the car, her face is etched with confusion and defiance. She doesn't understand why she's here, but now that she sees me, I can guess she's imagining no good will come from the meeting.

She walks woodenly toward the chalk circle. It's obvious she's trying her best to fight against the force pulling her there, but she's not stronger than the summoning spell. No one is. It's not until she comes to a stop in its center that she speaks.

"What are you doing here?" she spits. "I thought I told you to leave this town and never come back."

I flash a smile. "You told me to leave, but you never said I had to stay away."

She lunges for me but isn't able to connect. I'm standing outside the chalk circle, and she can't pass its boundary. She glares at me with a savagery I wouldn't have imagined possible the last time we met. She tried to act tough, but I could see right through her. She's different now. A smile curves my lips. "How's that Influence treating you?"

For a few moments, she doesn't respond. She's testing the invisible barrier penning her in, searching for weakness. When she finds none, a bit of the rage in her eyes abates. "Is that why you're here? You want to check up on me? Forgive me if I don't believe you're that altruistic. What do you care? It's your fault I'm like this anyway."

I hold up a finger. "Come on; that's not exactly true, now, is it? It's not my fault you're like this. That was your own—what was the word you used? Altruism. That had nothing to do with me. You could have simply allowed the Influence to take over your friends. It's what they were after. But you just couldn't let that happen. How's that working out for you?"

I can't quite read the look that flashes across her face. There's anger there, sure, but it's more than that. I can't imagine it's been easy adjusting to the Influence—especially not for someone like Krissa. She sees herself as a hero. Most accounts of people possessed by Influence don't describe the individuals with her kind of personality. Those who want to Influence are those who want power. All she wanted was to keep her friends safe. It's sad, really. But it's not my concern. Now that the Influence is within her, she's useful to me.

"Things are going well for the Amaranthine, by the way. Thanks for asking."

Krissa rolls her eyes. "Is that why I'm here? You want to give me an update? Guess what—I don't care. You and your coven could fall off the face of the earth and it wouldn't bother me in the least. You've already ruined my life; the least you can do is let me live it without your interference."

I do my best to paint on a wounded look. "I'm hardly here to interfere. I'm here to make an offer—something you'll surely want to take me up on."

She makes a circular motion with her hand, as if doing so can speed me along. "You might as well tell me because I'm pretty sure you won't let me go until I hear you out. I'll even save telling you no until after I've listened to what you have to say."

I like her fire. It's not something I got to see enough of last time

I was here. Sure, there was posturing about protecting her friends, but this is different. Now I know she really could back her claim. And I think she knows it, too. "Last time I was here, you killed my assassin. I don't know if you're aware, but traditionally the person who kills the assassin becomes the next one." I watch her, gauging her reaction.

But she's watching me, too. She waits for me to go on, and when I don't, she speaks. "Not interested."

"So quickly? I haven't even been able to tell you about our lovely benefits package."

She rolls her eyes. "I'm not looking for a career in the murder business, but thanks for the offer." She sweeps her hands around her. "I've heard you out; you can let me go now."

She's trying to pretend my offer doesn't intrigue her, but it doesn't take a psychic to see the flicker of interest in her eyes. "Sure, I'll let you go. You can go back to selecting a college and your classes and your major. Have you decided any of those things yet? Or are you going to follow your boyfriend to whatever university he chooses? Do you have any ideas about a major, or are you just going to throw a dart at a course catalogue? Or worse—do what your parents suggest?"

She glares at me, her face a mask of outrage—but that's all it is: a mask. She's trying to dredge up the appropriate indignation, but she's not managing. I'd bet money all my predictions are correct.

"I could give you so much more. The world is larger than you know. There are so many more things out there than you can even imagine, stuck here in Clearwater. You can be a part of it—a part of something special. Something great."

"I can be a murderer, you mean," she growls.

"I can give you an outlet for all that darkness inside you. Don't pretend you can't feel it. I know you can. I can see it in your eyes. Maybe you're able to hide it from family and friends, but not from me. You can't tell me this offer doesn't appeal to you—at least to part of you."

She stares at me for a moment before closing her eyes and shaking her head. "No. Not at all. Your offer is revolting, just like you. I don't want anything to do with it."

She says the words, but they lack conviction. It's almost like she's saying them because she knows she's supposed to, as if she's afraid someone is watching. She's a child telling the grownups what they want to hear. "You don't have to lie to me, Krissa. I know. Just be honest with yourself and—"

"I'd rather die than join you!" she screams.

Even through the spell's barrier, I feel the wave of rage emanating from her. This is the most convincing thing she's said so far. For a moment, I'm actually afraid she might make good on the threat. She has no weapon that I can see, but that doesn't mean she couldn't do herself harm if she really wanted to.

Would she really kill herself here and now? Usually, a person's innate sense of survival would keep her from doing something drastic, but this case is far from the usual. The Influence is making her more unstable than I anticipated. I'm not sure pushing her now wouldn't do more harm than good.

I take a step away from the barrier and hold my hands up in a gesture of surrender. "Don't do anything you can't undo."

She snarls like a caged animal, and I gulp. While it's true I've never dealt with someone filled with Influence before, I didn't imagine Krissa would be much different than Kai was. He was filled with the darkest soul I've ever encountered—until now. What's standing before me now isn't Krissa Barnette; it's the evil within her. For the first time, I question my wisdom in baiting her, in wanting her to become our assassin at all.

"I can see you need time to consider my offer," I say, keeping my voice as easy as possible. "No need to make any decisions right now."

Her eyes squeeze closed and her body twitches. I know before her gaze fixes on me again that she's trying to master herself. When I'm sure the lucid side of her can hear me, I produce a brown paper lunch bag from the pocket of my blazer. "I'm positive you'll change your mind about this, and when you do, I'll be waiting. You can use these items to summon me just as I've called you."

I set them on the ground outside the circle before pivoting and striding confidently toward my car. I'm behind the wheel before I send a small stream of water to break the chalk line. In my side mirror, I watch Krissa step across the boundary. She stares down at the bag for a long moment before kneeling and snatching it up.

I don't bother hiding my smile. She'll change her mind. She wants this—at least, part of her does. Once her two sides war about it, I have no doubt the Influence will win. And when it does, I'll return to the Amaranthine, triumphant. This will be all the proof I need that I truly deserve to be the next high priest.

All I have to do now is wait.

Chapter Ten
Krissa

I drum my fingers nervously on the arm of the couch. A kind of agitation grows in my stomach with each passing minute.

Tonight is the full moon.

Despite the fact that I wanted to keep things low-key, Jodi and Anya invited the whole circle plus the psychics to assist with the exorcism spell. I tried my hardest to endure the pep-talks each person seemed intent on giving me, but once Crystal arrived, I retreated to the sitting room.

I can't be in the same room with her—not after what I did. Part of me is afraid she'll remember somehow.

A bigger part of me fears I'll try to finish the job.

Owen laces his fingers with mine. "You scared?"

To his credit, this is the first time he's mentioned the spell today. Every time someone assures me it'll be okay, I get a sinking feeling in my stomach. It's not that I don't want to believe it—I do. It's just the more people try to convince me this will work, the more I fear it won't.

"What's to be scared of?" I ask, attempting to keep my voice light. "You guys are going to try to expel some nasty, evil energy from me—a power that could potentially fill any regular person it encounters before you manage to send it back to hell or wherever it came from. What could possibly go wrong?"

He squeezes my hand. "I'll be with you the whole time. I won't let anything happen to you."

I shift to face him. He's definitely scared; I can tell by the look in his eyes. But he's also resolved. While I don't know there's anything he could do if this spell goes sideways, it's obvious he means what he said. He'll protect me—of that I have no doubt.

I love him. The simple truth of it takes my breath away.

I've cared for Owen since I met him; I realized the depth of his importance to me when we weren't together in this timeline. But this is the first time I've known without a doubt that my feelings are more than infatuation, deeper than like.

I open my mouth, but the words stick in my throat. Can I tell him now? Maybe it's foolish, but I can't shake the feeling that telling him now, with the Influence still within me, would taint it somehow. And what if he's not ready to say it back? I don't want to force his hand simply because of what I'm about to undergo. And I don't want to distract him from everything he's supposed to be doing while the spell is cast.

It's not the right time for the words, but I can't keep my body from acting. I tilt my head and bring my lips to his. Owen returns my kiss, crushing my mouth with his. When he wraps a strong arm around my back and pulls me flush with his body, I wonder if he's allowing his actions to speak for him as well.

"Hey, Krissa, we're about to get—oh, my!"

Owen and I break apart and I turn toward the hall to find Jodi, her cheeks flushed and her hand over her heart. She squeezes her eyes closed and shakes her head. "Okay, then. I'd tell you to get a room, but I have a feeling your father would find that entirely inappropriate."

I sneak a glance at Owen, whose lips quirk at the corners. "Sorry, Jodi," I murmur in my best imitation of contrition.

She shakes her head again. "You'd better thank your lucky stars it was me and not your dad. I'm pretty sure he'd try to lock you away on the third floor," she mutters before motioning for us to follow her.

I keep Owen's hand in mine as we stand and walk down the hall. A quick glance inside the living room reveals the gang's all here. Even Elliot stands awkwardly beside the fireplace. I can't blame him for feeling ill at ease here in my house. While he did go out of his way to warn me about the true nature of Influence, that one act hasn't nullified his other choices. He was one of Seth's hand-picked minions, one of the strongest members of the Devoted. Anya trusts him implicitly, and while I'm willing to give him the benefit of the doubt, I know the same can't be said for the rest of my friends. From his spot in the armchair, Griffin all but glares in Elliot's direction. I make a mental note to ask him to dial back his hostility when this is over.

Provided, of course, that everything goes as planned.

The only face I don't see in the crowd is Sasha's, so when the door opens again, she's the one I expect to cross the threshold. But it isn't Sasha who enters the house; instead, Shelley Tanner and David Cole walk in. Jodi greets them warmly.

Heat builds in my stomach. When Jodi said she'd be calling in reinforcements, I had no idea she intended to include my principal and Crystal's former uncle by marriage. After the Influence spell, I didn't want to tell anyone who hadn't been in the clearing to see it happen. Jodi promised to keep the information on a need-to-know basis.

Apparently she lied.

Before Owen has a chance to stop me, I dart over to my aunt and pull her into the dining room. "What are they doing here?" I demand.

Jodi's eyes are wide. "Backup. I don't want to take any chances. I want all hands on deck for this spell."

"Did you tell them?" The Influence crackles in my veins and red begins to cloud my periphery. "Do they know what's going on with me?"

Jodi attempts to push my hand off her arm. "Krissa, you're hurting me."

My nails dig deeper into her flesh. How could she do this to me? She knows how uncomfortable I am involving all my friends in this. How could she go behind my back and invite the members of her old circle, too?

Hands close over my shoulders, and Owen spins me until I'm facing him. "Hey, calm down." His blue eyes pierce through the red encroaching on my vision. "Miss Tanner and Mr. Cole have helped before. I doubt Jodi told them the specifics. They're good friends. All they want to do is help you. That's all any of us wants to do."

I inhale deeply, and as I exhale, I'm able to pry my fingers from Jodi's arm. She rubs the spot and a wave of guilt washes over me, drowning out the sizzle of Influence. I grimace. "I'm so sorry."

She shakes her head. "I'll just be happy when this spell is over—when we've got you back."

I want to say more, to make her accept my apology, but before I can, she's crossed the hall into the living room and is calling for people's attention.

Owen brushes his fingertips along my jaw. "You ready?"

"Almost." I grab the front of his shirt in my fist and pull him down to meet my lips.

Owen accepts the kiss and returns it eagerly. I know Jodi is waiting for us to join her, but I don't care. I need this. Owen keeps me centered, keeps me sane. I need to feel like myself if I'm going to stand any chance of staying calm going into the spell.

It's only when Jodi clears her throat that the two of us break apart. I'm aware of everyone's eyes on us, but while Owen's cheeks tinge pink, mine stay cool. I'm not embarrassed. I don't care. I want the Influence pushed as far from my consciousness as possible before submitting myself to be exorcised, and if I need to be close to Owen to accomplish that, I'm not going to let anyone make me feel bad about it.

We cross the hall, hands linked, and find a spot beside Anya. Jodi is explaining to everyone what we hope to accomplish, and I'm grateful she skirts around the exact reason the spell is necessary. Maybe she didn't tell Shelly and David after all.

Owen bends down, placing his lips close to my ear. "Do you think he'll ever stop looking at me like that?"

I'm about to ask what he's talking about, but then I glance up and catch a glimpse of Fox. Fox's stormy eyes flick to Jodi, but not fast enough to keep me from knowing who he was looking at seconds before. He was watching me and Owen, and there are still traces of jealousy etched on his face.

"I get that things are complicated, but I don't see how he's having such a hard time with you moving on when he already has." Owen releases my hand and slides his arm around my waist.

"I could talk to him if you think it would help," I offer, even though the thought of broaching such a topic is about as unappealing as one-on-one study sessions with Mr. Martin. I have no idea how I'd start that particular conversation. Fox knows I'm not the same girl he dated for three years, but it has to be hard to see me with someone else. My alternate self was so closely linked with Fox for so long, I can't exactly blame him for having mixed feelings about me and Owen.

"I don't think that's necessary," Owen murmurs.

I probably should be paying attention to Jodi, but now that Fox is on my radar, I can't keep myself from glancing in his direction every so often. Dana stands beside him, her body turned toward his and pressing every available inch of her skin toward him. I wonder if she's sensed his jealousy. Even if I don't talk with him, maybe I should chat with her. The whole time I was trying to help her and Crystal get their abilities back, Dana was uneasy around me. I didn't really pick up on it at the time because I was so distracted, but now, when I think back, I remember how she tensed up any time Fox's name came up. She's pleasant when we cross paths now, but I'm not sure if she thinks I'm mad at her for telling him my secret, or if she still sees me as some kind of rival for his affection. Either way, it might do her some good to hear from me that neither is true.

Dana glances in my direction and catches me watching them. Her face tenses and she immediately looks away, but she also grabs Fox's arm and attempts to put it around her waist. Is she trying to mirror Owen and me? Fox tugs his arm from her grasp and the arm of his long-sleeve T-shirt pulls up for an instant. For a moment, a bracelet is visible on his wrist.

"How long has he been wearing that?" Owen asks quietly. "It looks a lot like the one you wear."

I noticed it, too. Although I barely caught a glimpse of it, it appeared almost identical. The hemp fibers seemed to be woven with Apache tears and snowflake obsidian—the same stones in my bracelet. I wear it now as an extra safeguard to keep other people from having to experience the Influence, but why would Fox wear a similar one? "Maybe he doesn't like the idea of Dana being able to read his thoughts," I suggest. "When he was with the other me, I don't think he knew about her psychic side. I'm not even sure she knew about it—she may have just thought everything she could do came from her magic."

Before Owen can respond, there's movement in the room. Jodi must have given some direction I didn't hear.

Anya places her hand on the small of my back and leads me toward the center of the room. Griffin and West stand on either end of the coffee table and lift it before carrying it out of the room. Bridget, Lexie, Bria, and Tucker collect small paper bags from the ledge of the fireplace. Other people shift around, clearly unsure where they should be standing for the moment. I take one last look around. Dana and Fox move toward Crystal. Felix stands close to the couch, rubbing the back of his neck uneasily. Shelly and David stand off to the side, chatting in low voices. Elliot lurks near Jodi, seeming not to want to get too close to anyone else. Almost everyone in Clearwater with any kind of ability is here in my living room, with one notable exception.

I glance at Anya. "Where's Sasha? Did she have something going on today?" I can't imagine that's the case. With all the time she's been putting into figuring out a way to help, it's hard to believe she wouldn't assist during an actual spell.

Anya tenses. "It's her fault we're here in the first place. It's her fault the Influence is inside you. Why on earth would you want her here now?"

I chew on my lower lip. Sasha has told me time and again she doesn't want Anya knowing she's helping me, but I still don't fully understand why. It's especially hard to keep the secret now with the heavy disappointment in Anya's voice. I don't know why it matters so much to me, but I want her to know her sister is trying to make things right. Obviously, it doesn't excuse what she's done, but none of us is perfect. What should count most is what we do moving forward.

Anya doesn't seem to expect a response. She points to the floor and helps me get into position. It's an odd sensation, lying down while everyone around me stands. I feel small and vulnerable. Energy thrums in my veins and I take a deep breath, hoping I can control it. I don't need the Influence rearing its head right now. Without sitting up, I scan the faces surrounding me until my eyes land on Owen. He stands at my head, but even upside down, the sight of him is calming.

Jodi, standing at my feet, begins murmuring a familiar incantation. I recognize it from when we performed this same spell on Crystal months ago. I close my eyes, willing myself to relax and believe that when this is over, everything will be back to normal.

A rueful smile tugs at the corners of my mouth. I'm not even sure what normal will look like for me after this. Preparing for senior year and applying to colleges? Making long-term plans with

Owen?

As much as I hate to admit it, Brody was spot on with what he said. I have no idea what I want to do with my life. If I do go to college, what will my major be? If I go, will I come back to Clearwater and take over the shop when Jodi is ready to retire? She mentioned to me once that the store would pass to me one day if I wanted it. But is that what I want for my life? Will I settle in this town, come back to this house, live out my days here in the place where everyone knows everyone else's business? Will I make teas and tinctures for the citizens of Clearwater, raise my own family, and teach my children to do the same? Will my life ever be anything more than it is now?

What if I want something bigger? Something greater? Can Owen give that to me? Can I even achieve it myself?

And what would that look like? I could travel the world, I suppose. But will that make me happy? I'm not sure. I don't know what I want out of my life, and suddenly it seems very important to know.

Images flash through my mind from the night of the Influence spell. After its power filled me, the Amaranthine assassin threatened the lives of my friends. Kai shot off spell after spell, but I deflected them easily. I met each of his blasts with one of my own, and when it came down to it, I was victorious. The energy that surged through me was exhilarating, like nothing I've ever experienced before. I felt entirely limitless, unbound by anything—including the restrictions of society.

I never felt guilty for killing Seth, but I was ashamed that I couldn't dredge up the emotion. It never even occurred to me to feel bad about incinerating Kai. On the contrary, I haven't spent a single moment lamenting what I did to him. He thought he was so strong, but I proved he wasn't. He was no match for me, for what resides inside me.

I was stronger. I am stronger. Stronger than anyone—or I could be. My power's locked away. The enchantment on my ring limits the Influence. But if I could access it fully, no one would stand in my way. If I joined the Amaranthine, no one would stand in their way. I would see to that. If people tried to stand against them, I could stop them. I could stop anyone.

I'm partially aware of the changing voices surrounding me, but their words have no meaning. It's just meaningless sound, white noise, like waves lapping on a beach. I'm floating, drifting. The thrum of the Influence that has been constantly buzzing below the surface is gone. There's nothing now—no feeling, just soft oblivion. I'm weightless. I'm nothing. I'm a soul untethered.

I'm free.

A weight settles in my stomach, shocking my system. The floating sensation from moments ago evaporates and it's as if I'm being pulled backwards, yanked down. Gravity seems to have more force than usual. I'm a magnet being drawn to another, stronger magnet. And when I crash back to reality, I long for my brief reprieve. The crackling in my veins is stronger than usual. The Influence singes and burns the inside of my body. Then the voices return, but they are no longer murmuring an incantation. These sounds are loud, sharp, and angry.

I blink my heavy eyelids several times before the room comes into focus. Everything is in motion. I try to focus on the voices, but it takes several seconds before language begins to make sense again.

"You said this would work! You said the worst that would happen was it would fight and we could try again." Jodi stands dangerously close to Anya, her face inches from the shorter woman's. "How do you explain what just happened?"

"First of all, I never guaranteed this was a sure thing," Anya snaps. "You had all the same information I did, and you chose to go through with this. Don't try to put the blame on me. You know I'm trying just as hard as you are to help her."

Owen places a hand on each woman's shoulder and turns them to face him. "You said you took every precaution. That's why we waited until the full moon. That's why we invited everyone we knew to help. How could you let this happen?" His voice is low and dangerous.

"It would've worked if everyone was pulling their weight," Griffin snarls argumentatively.

Felix rankles. "What are you trying to say?" In two steps, he's crossed to where Griffin stands.

If Griffin is uncomfortable with Felix's proximity, his posture belies it. "What I'm saying, psychic, is maybe if some people weren't too distracted standing next to their girlfriends to put in the energy required—"

"Now I know you're talking about your brother and not me, because there's nothing I wouldn't do to make Krissa right again," Felix growls.

Dana and Lexie throw themselves into the fray, but I don't register what they're saying. The angry sounds reach my ears, and the oppressive rage that pushes on me is so strong I don't need psychic abilities to sense it.

The snap and sizzle of the Influence within me is sharper and stronger than before. Their unsuccessful attempt at exorcising it from me only seems to have given it power, more energy to fight for dominance of my body.

I need to get away. I can't be in this room with all this fighting for much longer, or I'll lose control completely. I'm not sure if it's due to whatever just happened to me or not, but my body refuses to obey what my brain commands. I need to get up, to walk out to the porch, but I can't. An even stronger pull keeps me rooted to my spot, and every second I sit here, the pressure in my veins builds. My hands begin to itch with the barely suppressed urge to use the Influence. If the people in this room want mayhem, I'll be more than happy to oblige.

Tendrils of red smoke curl in my periphery. Images flicker in my mind's eye of all the spells I could do to silence everyone in this room. I could sever vocal cords with a snap of my fingers, break necks with a flick of my wrist. I could conjure fire to make its way up the legs of the ones who have betrayed me.

More red smoke rolls in, completely blocking out my vision, but as it does, one voice rises above the cacophony. There's something different about it. It's not angry like the rest. There's a note of pleading in it that cuts through the dark visions forming in my mind.

"Krissa? Can you hear me? Come back." The voice is close, but I'm having a hard time discerning what direction it's coming from. Hands cup my shoulders and twist me around to face the speaker.

It's Owen. It has to be. I still can't see through the red haze, but who else can calm me like this? I blink, hoping with each blink of my eyelids that my vision will clear and I'll see the face of the person I need more than anyone else.

"Are you okay?" the voice continues. The cadence is familiar, of course, but there's something off about it. It doesn't sound like Owen.

I press the heels of my hands against my eyelids, drawing in and releasing a deep breath before removing them. When I open my eyes, a jolt of surprise courses through me. It's not Owen standing in front of me, it's Fox.

I take a step backward, not because he's touching me or because he's so close, but because I'm trying to make sense of what's going on. When did I stand up? I was still lying on the floor when I came to. How much time has passed? Fear twists my stomach as I hastily survey the room. Did I do one of those things I imagined? But there's no damage, no carnage, only somewhat bewildered looks on the faces of those surrounding me. I turn back to Fox. "What happened?"

"It didn't work," he murmurs, stepping into the void between us.

70

"The psychics realized it wasn't the Influence that was being cast out, and we stopped the spell before things went too far. Then people started arguing, and you got up. You had this look in your eye..." He shakes his head.

Shame settles like a stone in the pit of my stomach. "Thank you for getting through to me."

He reaches for me and takes my hand. When he squeezes my fingers, he provides me with the strength I need to say what I have to say next.

"It didn't just not work. The spell... Things are worse. It's stronger now. The Influence. It's fighting harder for control."

Jodi rounds on Anya again. She opens her mouth and points a finger, but before she can start yelling, she seems to think better of it. With obvious effort, she drops her hand and releases the tension in her shoulders before continuing. "It seems this spell had more dangers than you anticipated," she says through gritted teeth.

Before Anya can defend herself, I break in. I can't have them blaming each other when I know the truth. It's my fault for not telling them. "I think it was just a matter of time. I haven't wanted to admit it to anyone—even to myself, really—but it's been getting stronger every day for a while now." I drop my eyes as I say it, unwilling to witness the fear and horror that are undoubtedly brimming in the eyes of everyone present.

A hand brushes beneath my chin, inviting me to look up. Fox's stormy eyes meet my gaze. "We'll figure this out."

I want to believe him. I want to think there's some spell out there, waiting to be discovered, that will rid me of this darkness. Looking at Fox now, I can almost trust it's true.

Jodi sighs, and it takes everything in me to ignore the fact that it sounds like defeat. "I guess we're going back to the drawing board."

She says it as if it's so simple. Maybe for her it is. She doesn't know what's going on inside me, the constant battle between me and the Influence. I hope they find a solution soon, before she's forced to learn just how real my struggle is.

Chapter Eleven
Brody

Though lacking in ambiance, the diner on the edge of town has surprisingly decent food. I ate at more than my share of dives last time I was in Clearwater. It's rarely the big chain restaurants with the best selections; usually, I find the most delicious dishes at hole-in-the-wall establishments that are kept alive not by the loyalty of regular patrons, but by that special spark of genius possessed by a chef.

This is not one of those places, but the food is good enough that I'm back. I've even carved out a regular spot, although it's unlikely anyone in the restaurant has noticed: I find it's easier to cast glamors and pose as a different person each time I visit. Doing so keeps the waitresses from trying too hard at small talk.

But I'm using no magic to conceal myself tonight. My mind is far too busy to bother with such tricks.

Jade is already asking for a progress report.

I received the text message an hour ago and I still haven't responded. What am I supposed to say? I figured I'd have more time before she demanded an update. I've only been here just over a day.

Typically, reports are nothing to agonize over. When I dealt with the Crystal Jamison situation, Jade wasn't nearly so interested in my daily progress—and that was related to information the Amaranthine had been seeking for generations.

This is because of Lena. I can feel it. She's there, whispering in Jade's ear, prompting her to doubt me.

That's why my response has to be perfect.

A turkey club sits, untouched, on its plate as I pick up my phone from its spot by the water glass. After a few swipes on the screen, I begin typing a message detailing how I'm tracking Krissa's movements and gathering intel. Should I mention I've already spoken with her? On the one hand, revealing that information will show I'm not wasting time. On the other, it could be used against me, since I wasn't immediately able to persuade her to join us.

My thumbs hover over the screen. The truth or a lie? Which will cast me in the best light?

Someone moves into my periphery, standing too close to be another patron. Assuming it's my waitress—Sue, according to her nametag—I wave my hand dismissively. "I don't need anything right now." I reposition my grip on the phone, but before I can continue typing, the person slides into the booth across from me.

I look up, ready to read the waitress the riot act for disrupting my meal, but when my gaze falls on the booth's new occupant, I'm too surprised to say anything.

"What are you doing here?" Sasha demands. She looks just as I remember her: petite but strong, with thick dark hair and self-assured posture. Even the fire in her eyes is the same as it was during our last encounters. "You got what you wanted, didn't you? Why are you back in Clearwater?"

A smile spreads itself across my lips. She's feisty, I'll give her that. Her spark didn't escape me during my first trip here. It's obvious that where she grew up, she was the strongest witch she knew. She has a fearlessness about her borne of confidence that her strength is unrivaled. Her swagger is, of course, laughable. She's not nearly as strong as she thinks she is, and one day she'll learn that. "Why I'm here doesn't concern you. You and your family aren't on my radar this visit, if that's what you're worried about.

You kept up your end of the bargain, and I'm nothing if not a man of my word. You can run along now."

She bristles. "I won't be dismissed like a child. This is my town, and I have a right to know what you're doing in it."

I chuckle. "Oh, it's your town now, is it? Are you the new self-appointed savior? I suppose there's an opening now that the old one is being ravaged by the darkness you invited here. Tell me, Sasha—how sweet is your revenge?" I savor the slight widening of her eyes as she registers my words. "Don't look so surprised. Of course I knew what you were doing. I knew from our first meeting that you had no interest in helping the Amaranthine. But your interests served mine, so I didn't care that you intended to use me. Now, I recommend you go about your day and forget you ever saw me."

She squares her shoulders in a valiant effort to look unfazed. "And if I don't? What—are you going to have your assassin kill me?" Her lips curl. "Oh, wait."

I lean across the table, no longer in any mood to deal with her. "It's true, I'd much rather have someone else do my dirty work, but make no mistake—I could kill you as easily as breathing, Sasha. Don't make me prove it."

Her eyebrows twitch almost imperceptibly, and a muscle in her jaw jumps. I'm pretty sure she's finally realizing she's not the biggest bully on the playground. At the very least, she seems to be deciding she doesn't want to test me right now. After a beat, she stands and leaves without another word.

Sue, the waitress, arrives as Sasha brushes past her. "Will your friend be coming back?" she asks, water glass in hand.

"No," I say, and Sue doesn't ask the question stirring in her eyes. She backs away quickly, leaving me to finish the task I started.

I delete the text I began. It's fortuitous Sasha found me when she did. Ten minutes ago, I had no idea how to respond to Jade, but now I'm feeling more like myself than I have in days. I have no doubt my assured tone will come through in my words.

I've made contact. I'm confident she'll accept my offer. She just needs a little time.

Chapter Twelve
Krissa

When I wake the next morning, I'm sore in a way I didn't even know was possible. My muscles are weak, and sitting up in bed brings a wave of dizziness. It's as if I've just gotten over a bad bout of the flu.

The last thing I want to do today is go to school. I grab my phone off my bedside table with a half-formed notion of texting Felix to see if he'd like to play hooky brewing in my mind. But the thought is chased from my head when I see the notifications on my lock screen. Sasha has sent me no fewer than five texts since last night.

A wave of guilt floods me, roiling my already uneasy stomach. Did she find out about the spell? Is she mad because she wasn't invited? I dismiss the thoughts immediately: Not being involved is partially her choice. But maybe she somehow got wind of how badly the exorcism failed. Anya could have reached out to her after I asked why she wasn't present, and maybe Sasha's upset I didn't at least tell her what we were planning before I went through with it.

I read through Sasha's messages. They're vague, but the takeaway is simply that she needs to see me. She's been waiting for a response since last night, so I quickly type one out. I offer to meet up with her later today, but in an immediate text back, she insists we meet ASAP.

I take my time getting ready, mostly because my body seems completely incapable of rushing. By the time I make it downstairs, there's noise and movement coming from the kitchen. Mom, Dad, and Jodi buzz around the room, each in the middle of their own morning routine. Dad is cooking enough scrambled eggs to feed an army, Mom is cutting fruit, and Jodi stands at the counter with a half-dozen different bowls of herbs before her.

Mom notices me first. A worried expression flickers across her face, and I wonder how much of what happened last night Jodi relayed to her. "You feeling okay, honey? You look a little pale."

"I've been better." I don't want to make her worry any more than I know she already is, so I don't elaborate.

Dad offers a smile over his shoulder. "I'm making eggs," he announces, as if I haven't noticed.

I shake my head. The thought of ingesting any kind of food is too much for me to handle. "Actually, I'm meeting Owen for bagels this morning," I lie.

Dad's face falls, but he rebounds quickly. "Okay, more for me."

Jodi edges past him, a stainless steel travel mug in her hand. "Drink this. It should help you feel better."

I don't bother asking what is in this morning's tea. It doesn't really matter as long as it works. "Thank you."

Before I can turn back to the hall, mom crosses to me in two steps and wraps me in a hug. The embrace lasts longer than usual, like she's afraid she won't have many more chances to hold me. The thought makes my eyes prickle, but I blink the tears back. I don't want her to see me cry. I don't want her to think she has to be strong for both of us.

Less than ten minutes later, I'm pulling into the parking lot of the bagel shop Felix and I once visited. Sasha's Civic is already there. When I climb out of my car, I'm sure to bring my travel cup. Although I've only had a few sips of the concoction, my strength is already returning. While I don't think this blend of herbs will make me feel one hundred percent better, I have a feeling it will get me close.

Sasha is sitting at a table in the back of the restaurant. A paper cup rests on the table, but she doesn't touch it. Her expression is a mix of anger and concern. Now I'm really curious.

"What's up?" I ask as I settle in the chair across from her.

She studies me in her shrewd way. She's not a psychic, but she's very good at reading people. I wonder what she sees in my face this morning. "I have news. You're not going to like it."

My stomach sinks. Is it something about the Influence? Has she confirmed I'm a lost cause? I'm not ready to hear that if it's the case. I take another sip of my tea.

"I went out to get something to eat last night, and I saw someone I hoped to never see again. I hate to be the bearer of bad news, but Brody is back in town. I didn't get a clear sense of what he wanted, but I'm sure it can't be good."

I exhale, some of the tension draining from my shoulders. The news isn't anything I can't handle. "I know, and I know why he's here."

Her eyes narrow. "You knew he was here and you didn't tell me?"

Her tone puts me on the defensive. "I was hoping he'd leave when I turned him down. Besides, I don't have to tell you everything."

A wounded expression flickers across her face, replaced almost immediately by an irritated one. "I never said you did, but a little warning would have been nice. Last time he was here, he threatened my family. If he's back, I need to make precautions to be sure they're safe."

I understand where she's coming from, but her concern is unnecessary. Given the reason for his visit, why would he threaten Anya or Elliot again? "I have it handled," I say, even though it's not entirely true. I told Brody I wasn't interested, but despite my hope, I never expected he would simply pick up and leave town. It doesn't surprise me he's still here, but when I don't contact him, he'll surely get the hint.

Sasha tilts her head. "You going to tell me why he's here?"

I haven't told anyone about Brody's arrival, so I haven't been able to talk to anyone about his offer. Since Sasha already knows he's here, I don't see the harm in giving her the reason. "Job offer. He wants me to be the new Amaranthine assassin." I roll my eyes to illustrate how ridiculous I find the idea.

Sasha doesn't smile. "And you seriously think he's going to give up because you said no the first time he asked? Maybe you're having a hard time remembering because you weren't directly on the receiving end, but last time he was in town, Brody didn't take no for an answer. If threatening you doesn't work, he'll go after the people you love. And if warnings don't work, he'll hurt them. I have no doubt about that."

Her assertions make me shiver. With everything else going on, I haven't given much thought to the lengths Brody might go to in order to convince me to join him.

Unbidden, a series of images and sensations flashes through my mind. I remember what it was like the night I battled Kai. He was cocky. He boasted about all the people he killed, and for the first time, I wonder how he did it. Was he straightforward, or did he take his time? Did he make elaborate plans, or go straight for the kill? Did people see him and tremble, knowing they were looking into the face of death? Is that how they would look at me if I were to take his place?

I close my eyes and shake my head. No, no one will ever look at me that way, because I'll never become that person. "He'll have to accept my answer once we get the Influence out of me."

Sasha blows out a breath. "I'm not having much luck on that front. There's the dissevering spell, like I mentioned before, but beyond that, I've got nothing. Short of killing you, I have no new ideas."

I know she's not serious, but talk of my death sends a shiver down my spine. I'm reminded of the other day when Felix made the same macabre joke. "Yeah, Jodi and Anya aren't having much better luck."

She leans across the table. "Have they come up with anything?"

I bite the inside of my cheek. I should tell her about what happened yesterday, but I'm not sure how she'll react. Still, she deserves to know. "We tried a spell last night. An exorcism." I hold up my hands and shrug. "Didn't work."

Her eyebrows arch. "It's actually not a bad idea," she says thoughtfully. "I wonder if maybe you just need more power."

I shake my head. "I don't think that'll work."

"But did they really give it their all? I mean, I get that they were channeling the full moon, but maybe there weren't enough witches to do the spell. Let me guess: Jodi, Lexie, Griffin." She ticks off each one on her fingers.

"Not just the witches. We had the psychics, too. Everyone was there."

Sasha's face tightens and I realize a moment too late that I've said the wrong thing. "Everyone?" Her tone is a challenge. It's obvious she's dubious we had enough power to properly work the spell.

I know she won't let me off the hook without giving her all the details, and I'm not up for a fight at the moment. I list off all the people who were at the house last night. None of the names surprise her until I get to Shelley Tanner and David Cole, but it's not until I drop Elliot's name that her eyes go wide.

"Elliot?" Her eyebrows hike up her forehead. "And no one had a problem with that?"

I shake my head. "Everyone knows he's the one who warned Anya and me about the Influence spell. Anya vouches for him." I press my lips together before continuing. "I asked her why you weren't there, for what it's worth."

"Oh, really?" she asks with an air of nonchalance. "What'd she say?"

I could kick myself. Why did I have to bring it up? "She's still angry," I say quietly. "If you'd just let me tell her that you're helping, maybe—"

She shakes her head. "No. I don't want her to feel like she has to be nice to me because I'm helping you. I want her to actually forgive me because she wants to, because I'm her sister."

"She will," I say automatically. I'm not sure if it's true, but I want it to be, for Sasha's sake.

After a beat, she makes a show of checking the time on her phone. "You should get going. You don't want to be late for school."

I open my mouth, but before I can say anything, Sasha stands and walks away from the table.

I'm not sure why I care so much. She's done plenty of terrible things. All I know is that if she can be a better person, then no one is beyond redemption.

Chapter Thirteen
Fox

There's a substitute in third-hour English class, and I'm glad for it. Even on my best days, English isn't one of my favorite subjects, and today is definitely not one of my best days.

I'm still shaken by last night's spell. What would've happened if Felix and Tucker hadn't called out when they did? From my perspective, the spell had been going well. I felt the swell of energy as our incantation did its work. I knew we were pulling a spirit from Krissa's body. I had no idea it wasn't the Influence we were expelling.

I could have lost her forever. I fought the urge to go to her as soon as the spell was over. I could have—everyone else was distracted enough. But once I saw in her eyes something was wrong, I couldn't fight it anymore. She needed me, and I didn't care who saw it.

I've already taken more than a little crap from Dana for my interaction with Krissa after the spell was over. She was sullen on the way home, and she even had the audacity to tear up when she asked why I held Krissa's hand for so long. When I snapped at her for being so jealous, she actually cried.

The tardy bell rings, and the substitute—a decent-looking twenty-something guy in a button-down shirt and wire-rimmed glasses, stands and starts calling out names to take attendance. Once I verify I'm here, I open my notebook and start drawing.

When we were dating, Krissa always encouraged me to grow as an artist. That's what she called me: an artist. I never really thought of myself that way. I just like to draw. But Krissa would ask me regularly what I was working on. She would point out parts that she liked particularly well and she'd ask how I managed different effects. Dana, on the other hand, has only ever complained when I pull out my notebook, insisting I should be talking with her instead.

How did I ever end up in this situation? Dana is a pretty awful girlfriend. She's too needy, too clingy. Of course, I know why I started dating her. For all her faults, she has a number of attributes. She told me the truth when Krissa kept it from me. She was a compassionate ear when I wanted to rage about how unfair it all was. And I'd be lying if I said part of her allure isn't physical. She is, hands down, one of the hottest girls in school. After Krissa started getting cozy with Owen, I wanted to prove to myself—to her, to anyone watching—that I had moved on, too.

Except I never did. And neither did Krissa.

Once the sub finishes with attendance, he points to the white board and reads off the instructions the teacher left there, as if we couldn't do the same ourselves. We're supposed to answer some questions about the novel we just finished in preparation for the discussion we'll have tomorrow in class. When he's recited the directions, he calls on a couple girls in the front of the room to pass out the paper with the topics on it. I roll my eyes as both girls toss their hair and giggle in an obvious attempt to flirt with him.

Once the questions have been passed out, the sub settles behind the teacher's desk and pulls out his phone. The room comes alive in a flurry of movement as my classmates decide this particular substitute won't mind if they sit by their friends.

I flip the discussion question sheet over and start sketching a dragon. The buzz in the classroom grows as everyone starts talking at once, and I do my best to tune out the voices. When someone grabs the empty desk in front of mine, I don't think anything of it—

until it gets turned around and pressed against mine.

Owen raises his chin in greeting. "Can I sit?" He doesn't wait for my permission.

I tense. Before he started remembering the other reality, I wouldn't have thought anything of him coming over to chat. We were never close friends, but we were more than acquaintances. We even partnered up on assignments from time to time earlier this year. But since everything changed, he's given me a wide berth. So why is he here now? Has he figured something out? I shouldn't have taken Krissa's hand last night. It felt so natural in the moment. She obviously needed someone to comfort her, and I was the one who noticed it—not Owen. Did I cross the line?

Once he's seated, Owen stares at me for a moment before taking in a breath. "I wanted to say thank you."

Instead of putting me at ease, his words make the hair at the back of my neck stand up. "What for?"

He offers the smallest of smiles. "You were the one to talk Krissa down last night. I didn't see she was getting worked up. I should've been the one to notice."

Damn right he should've been the one to notice. I fight against saying it out loud. Owen's not being confrontational, and I don't want to start a fight. "Of course, man. Anything for Krissa." I'm about to leave it at that, but I just can't help myself. "When you're with someone for three years, you get to know their expressions pretty well. I get how you could've missed it." It's totally a dick thing to say, but the whole situation chafes. Of course I'm the one who realized Krissa needed help. I know her better than Owen ever could.

His eyebrows draw together, and for a second I wonder if I've gone too far. But when he leans across his desk, his expression is more conspiratorial than pissed. "You know I know, right? About the other reality? I know she's not the girl you dated. You don't have to pretend with me."

I study his face, trying to determine whether it's his turn to be an asshole. I decide it's not exactly in his nature, but still, I can't stand the idea of him thinking he's won, that my time with her doesn't count. "I know you know. But despite the fact that she's different, there's still so much of her that's the same. I can still read her. I know her expressions better than I know my own." I hesitate before pressing on. "Whether you like it or not, I still care about her."

Owen rubs the back of his neck—uncomfortable, but not angry. "I know that. And I get how things are screwed up. Believe it or not, I understand how hard this is for you."

I'm about to ask him how he can possibly know, but the answer comes to me on its own. Before Krissa and I started dating three years ago, she and Owen were pretty close to getting together. She broke his heart to prove her loyalty to Crystal and the circle. For the first time, I wonder how hard it was for Owen to watch her move on and be with me.

"I just wanted to tell you how much I appreciate that you're still willing to be there for her even after everything that's happened. Believe it or not, your friendship means a lot to Krissa. I'm glad she can count on you."

My mind spins with a thousand responses. Indignation bubbles in the pit of my stomach. I hate sitting here while he plays the dutiful boyfriend. He's clueless. He has no idea what's going on. I know more about Krissa than he ever will. I want to tell him that. I want to take him down a peg or two, but before I get the chance, a riot of laughter breaks out in the back of the classroom. The sub looks up for the first time in minutes, seemingly surprised to find there are still students in the room. He sets down his phone and stands long enough to call over the noise for everyone to return to their assigned seats or he'll start sending people to the office.

Despite the fact that his threat is very possibly idle, Owen stands and moves his desk back to its original position before returning to his assigned spot. I watch him as he opens his copy of the novel and starts working on the assignment. The anger from a moment ago dissipates, replaced by a twinge of guilt. He really has no idea. As much as I've wanted to hate him, he's actually a pretty decent guy, and I can't pretend that what Krissa and I are doing in secret won't hurt him when it comes to light.

I wish I knew why she's so intent on keeping our relationship quiet. I get that she cares for him, but she can't be with both of us— not in the long term. As much as the truth sucks, it's necessary. And I know firsthand how much more a secret hurts the longer it's kept.

Chapter Fourteen
Krissa

I moan, pressing my hand to my stomach as Owen opens the door of the pizzeria. "Why did you guys let me eat that much?"

"Let you?" Lexie scoffs as we spill onto the sidewalk. "I've tried to get between you and food before and nearly lost my hand. I'm not risking life and limb to convince you not to eat one more piece of pizza."

Owen slips his arm around my waist, and Felix links hands with Lexie as we start up Main Street toward Wide Awake Cafe. The four of us planned this date night earlier this week, but after the failure with the spell on Wednesday, Lexie suggested we cancel. I was the one who insisted we not break our plans. I need normal activities like this. Times like these, I can forget about the Influence and its hold on me. I can convince myself I have a regular life.

Almost.

"We still haven't decided what game we're playing," Felix reminds us as we make our way toward the coffee shop. All through our meal, he pushed for Apples to Apples, but Lexie kept insisting the psychics would have an unfair advantage.

"I've already given you my choice," Lexie says.

Felix tips his head back and groans as they pass the door to the bakery. "I'm so not in the mood for Jenga."

Lexie tugs his hand to keep him on pace with her. "You're not in the mood to get your ass kicked, you mean."

A smile curves my lips as I listen to their banter. While the two of them are walking at a decent clip, Owen and I make no effort to keep up with them. The late spring sunshine beats down, warming me in a way I tend to forget is possible during the long winter months. With Owen's arm around me, I'm able to pretend our lives are unencumbered by the events of the past fall and winter.

The bakery door swings open in front of us and a customer rushes out, a cake box balanced in his hands. He doesn't look where he's going and nearly collides with Owen, who hastily helps steady the box in the guy's hands before it has a chance to fall to the ground.

"Sorry about that. Thanks, man."

I'm so distracted by all the action I don't recognize the guy until he speaks. Owen must have realized who he was at the same moment because he stiffens as I smile in greeting.

"Tucker! You're buying a cake?" I stare at the box, trying to determine if it could be holding something else. Buying baked goods is pretty out of character for him. I look to his face for a clue, but all I find there is a harassed expression. "You okay?"

Tucker blows out a breath, some of the tension draining from his shoulders as he does. "I'm fine. It's my mom's birthday and my stepdad was supposed to pick up the cake. I even checked with him earlier this week, and he promised to do it. But, here I am." He shakes his head. "There'll be hell to pay for the next year if that woman doesn't get cake on her birthday."

Owen and I both laugh, but it's the kind of perfunctory laughter that occurs when you're not sure if something's supposed to be funny or not. In all the time we spent together this winter, Tucker never really talked about his family. With as many hours as he put in at Griffin's apartment, I always assumed his home life was less than ideal. I wonder if his stepfather is always unreliable, and exactly what kind of "hell" would be in store for Tucker if he didn't bring her cake. Will his mom want them to spend time together? If so, I can't imagine Tucker is looking forward to it.

We haven't spent nearly as much time together these last few weeks. Part of it is because of the Influence spell, and part of it because I've been spending most of my spare time with Owen—but that's no excuse. It strikes me for the first time that I miss his company. "We're heading down to the coffee shop for some board game madness. If your family stuff ends early enough, you should come join us," I say as Felix and Lexie make their way back to us.

After a beat, Felix smiles. "Yeah, man. I'd be happy to kick your ass at Jenga."

The corners of Tucker's mouth twitch. "Thanks for the offer, but I think I'll wait until I've got a girlfriend to join in on your double dates." Before I can object, he raises his chin. "I'll catch you guys later."

Lexie's eyes follow him until he's out of earshot. When the four of us resume our course down the sidewalk, she speaks. "It's weird. I thought for sure he'd be back together with Crystal by now. Weeks ago, she had some elaborate plan to make up for lost time— whatever that's supposed to mean."

I bite my lower lip. Tucker told me about that night. He agreed to go out with Crystal mostly because she was so insistent, but when she floated the idea of getting back together, he turned her down. "He told me he wouldn't—couldn't—get back with her. Not now. Not after... everything that happened." I don't want to be thinking about the night of the Influence spell, so I shove the memories back down and force a smile. "He says being with her now would kind of feel like dating me, and he couldn't handle that."

Despite my efforts, red begins to creep into the corners of my vision. Flashes of that night play out in my mind's eye. He won't date Crystal because she has my magic. There's a piece of me inside her—one that doesn't belong, that she doesn't deserve.

It's only when Owen steps in front of me that I realize I've stopped walking. He searches my face as Lexie and Felix continue down the street. "He won't date Crystal because she has your magic?"

I blink, but it doesn't clear away all the red. "Yeah—kind of silly, I know."

He shakes his head. "No, it's not. He's a pretty loyal friend, isn't he?" I nod, and Owen smiles. "I promise I'll try harder to like him."

He leans forward and presses a kiss to my lips. He means it to be short and sweet, but when he tries to end it, I don't let him go. I lace my fingers behind his neck and pull him back to me. I'm rewarded with a crushing kiss that takes my breath away. His arms snake around my back and hold my body flush against his.

A catcall from a passerby makes Owen finally pull away. When I open my eyes, all traces of the red smoke are gone. I love the way Owen does that. I can't imagine how I would be getting through all this without him.

As we continue toward the cafe, I glance up and down Main Street to see if I can determine who disturbed us. But what catches my eye isn't a catcaller—it's a familiar form that makes the red rush back in to cloud my vision.

Brody.

He lurks in an alley between the pharmacy and the boutique owned by Lexie's mom. The Influence crackles just beneath my skin, but as it surges, I realize it's not aimed at Brody. I don't want to hurt him—I want to hurt someone else, anyone else, to prove myself to him.

I want him to see how capable I would be in the role of assassin.

A small voice in the back of my head reminds me that's not who I am. My vision is already reduced nearly to pinpricks, and I'm afraid what will happen when it goes entirely red. Before it can, I tug on Owen's arm and pull him back to me. I'm barely able to see the surprise in his eyes before I cover his mouth with mine. Even more so than moments ago, I need this—I need him. I need to be reminded of who I am and what's really important.

For a moment, Owen hesitates, but any reluctance soon fades and he's kissing me more fervently than before. I barely notice I'm moving until my back presses against the cool glass of whatever store we're standing in front of. I weave my fingers through the hair at the nape of his neck and do everything I can to live in this moment, in this kiss.

"Hey, why don't you two get a room?" Felix calls.

After another moment, Owen pulls away, the look in his eyes making it clear he'd like little more than to take Felix's advice. In this moment, I wouldn't say no. Without Owen, I'm afraid I'd lose myself to the Influence and not be able to find my way back.

His eyes stay locked on mine for another beat, long enough for me to understand he'd be happy to pick up where we left off at a later time. Then he slips his hand into mine and tugs me toward our friends.

As we go, it takes every bit of my concentration to keep from glancing in Brody's direction.

But I won't give in. I won't be his assassin.

Chapter Fifteen
Fox

There are still two weeks of school left before finals, and I'm already checked out.

Faking my way through a discussion about themes and character motivations in English left me mentally drained. I make my way to my locker to drop off the novel and notebook so I don't have to bring them down to the lunchroom. This should be my favorite time of the school day—time to relax and not have to think about things. But it's not. Dana has a hard time sitting in silence. She always has to be talking, and if I'm not responding, she insists I tell her what's wrong. She won't believe me if I tell her there's nothing.

I usually meet her at her locker before walking down to the cafeteria, but I can't bring myself to do it today. When she finally makes her way to our table, she'll probably bitch at me, but those first five minutes of silence might be worth it.

Instead of heading toward the common stairs that would take me past Dana's locker and to the lunchroom quickly, I head for a seldom-used flight at the opposite end of the building. If I'm going to take a walk alone, I might as well make the most of it.

I'm halfway down to the first floor when someone calls my name. I curse under my breath, but it's only Crystal. The fact that she's sought me out piques my curiosity, and I slow down to wait for her. "What's up?"

She twists her fingers together nervously—something I'm not

sure I've ever seen her do before. "I want to talk to you about something. It's been on my mind for a while now, and I've been considering who the best person to tell would be."

It's been a while since I talked with Crystal. The last time we were even in a room together was at Krissa's house the other night. She looks different from the girl I've come to know over the years—she wears less makeup, and her posture isn't as self-assured as it used to be. She used to be flanked by Bridget, Lexie, and Krissa at all times, but the three of them have split away from her. For the first time, I wonder what's going on in her life. I've been so caught up in my own, it's never crossed my mind to ask. What kind of a shitty friend does that make me? Or does our natural distance simply point to how flimsy our friendship was to begin with? "Don't leave me in suspense."

She presses her lips together and exhales through her nose. "I'm worried about Krissa."

"Newsflash," I mutter, continuing down the stairs. "Who isn't?"

She keeps pace with me. "No, that's not what I mean. Well, maybe it is."

I try to stay nonchalant, but the back of my neck begins to prickle. I'm not sure where she's going with this. I hold my breath until she continues.

"Has she seemed off to you?"

I consider her question. My first instinct is to tell her no. Krissa finally seems like herself—like the girl she's supposed to be in this reality. The two of us fit together like we haven't in months. But I can't tell her that. Crystal has no idea how much time I've been spending with Krissa, and I'm not about to let on. "Off how?"

We're on the first floor now, in the foyer outside the main office. It's not a spot where many students linger, but we stop. She leans against the wall and scans the vicinity to make sure we're not going to be overheard. Her caution is unnecessary—there's no one here. "Sometimes she kind of stares off into space and gets these looks like... I don't know how to describe it."

I could think of a hundred reasons why Krissa might get distracted or daydream, but obviously Crystal thinks this is more than that. "Well, she's got a lot going on right now. It's not surprising if she zones out sometimes. Have you talked to her about it?"

Crystal's eyes narrow like she's trying to remember something, but then a soft shiver overtakes her and her face goes blank for an instant. "I get the feeling she doesn't want to talk to me about it."

I study her, trying to figure out how such a simple question elicited such an odd reaction. "Why? I mean, besides the fact she doesn't seem to want to talk to anyone about, you know, not being a hundred percent."

She presses her lips together. "I don't know. I just... I guess I can't blame her if she doesn't want to talk Influence with me—not after what went down."

Now I'm the one who feels embarrassed. Any time I think about the day we did the Influence spell, I can't help looking at it from Krissa's point of view. She lost all her natural abilities that day only to be filled with the darkness that made her kill a man right in front of us. It's easy to disregard how the events of that day must make Crystal feel, because she got what she wanted—the ability to wield magic again. Is it possible Crystal is feeling guilty because of what happened? Does she blame herself for what happened to Krissa? "You're her friend. She cares about you—otherwise, she wouldn't have done what she did. It might do her good if you show her how much you care about her."

Crystal sighs. "Maybe you're right." She pushes off the wall and starts down the hall again. I follow, but we've made it no more than a dozen paces before a familiar clip-clop sound meets my ears. I fight the urge to curse again.

"Fox! There you are. When you didn't show up at my locker, I checked the lunchroom, but you weren't there either. I got worried."

Irritation flares in my abdomen, sending pinpricks of heat down my arms. She got worried about me? What the hell did she imagine was going to happen to me at school? It's not like there are trained assassins walking around here or something. "Crystal wanted to talk," I say shortly.

Dana's eyes go round. "Oh? What about?"

I glance at Crystal. I'm not sure if she wants to share her concern with anyone but me.

When neither of us responds, Dana crosses her arms over her chest. "Krissa. Of course."

"What do you mean, of course?" I ask, my voice sharper than I intend.

Dana's arms drop and she takes a half step back. "I just mean it's like we can't go five minutes without her coming up somehow. She's everyone's favorite topic of conversation."

"That's not fair," I say, annoyed by her obvious jealousy, even though it doesn't surprise me. "We're trying to help her. You should know *why* better than anyone."

Dana shifts in her high-heeled shoes, looking uncomfortable, and I know I've hit a nerve. "We should get moving. The hall monitor likes to sweep this area once the lunch bell rings. I saw her earlier today, and she's in a bad mood. I bet she's looking for any excuse to give someone detention."

Crystal bites her lower lip. "Thanks for the heads-up. I so don't need a detention right now." She casts an apologetic glance in my direction before heading back the way we came. I'm not sure whether she needs to hit her locker before going to lunch or if she just doesn't want to be involved in whatever drama is about to happen. I almost wish I could follow her.

I start toward the cafeteria, and Dana is at my side in an instant. She reaches for my hand, but I shake her off.

"What's wrong?" she asks, sounding wounded.

My irritation is getting the best of me. I know what I should do—what Krissa would want me to do. I should shrug off my mood and pretend like everything is okay. But I can't do it today. Keeping up appearances is taking its toll. "You know, I can't help but notice how comfortable you seem using those psychic abilities."

She draws back her shoulders. "I know what you're thinking," she grumbles. "I should thank my lucky stars and kiss Krissa's ass since she's the reason I'm psychic again."

I sigh, already regretting having brought it up. "That's not what I'm thinking."

Her shoulders droop and her mouth settles into a pout. "Well, it's my best guess since you're wearing that." She points at the hemp bracelet on my left wrist. "It's just like the one she wears."

It's just like Krissa's because she helped me make it, but I'm not going to tell Dana that. "I don't know why you're surprised it's similar. I doubt there are many spells that block a mind from being read. I knew this would work, so it's the spell I chose."

Dana crosses her arms over her chest, somehow managing to accentuate her bust in the process. There was a time when such a move would have distracted me, but not now. "I don't see why you need it."

There are so many reasons I don't want Dana reading my thoughts, but the thing that pushed it over the edge was Krissa's insistence on the secrecy surrounding our relationship.

Dana doesn't seem to expect me to respond. "You never needed something like that when you were dating her."

I stop walking. We're barely two yards from the commons, but I can't take another step. I'm so sick of this—so sick of Dana comparing every aspect of our relationship to the one I had with Krissa. I'm tired of her thinking the world revolves around her. "First of all," I begin as Dana turns to face me, "I didn't even know she was psychic. I didn't find that out until a few months ago. And second—not everything is about you. You didn't bitch about not being able to read my thoughts before Krissa sacrificed herself to the Influence. Just because you can get into my head now doesn't mean I want you there."

Her eyes are wide. I know I've hurt her, and deeply. But I don't give her a chance to reply. I storm into the commons, feeling only mildly guilty for what I've said. Maybe it makes me an awful person, but I can't take it anymore. Living this double life is getting too hard. Something needs to change.

Chapter Sixteen
Krissa

I find myself in the strange moments between sleep and wakefulness. Memories of a dream play just beyond my awareness. I think it was a good dream. I'm happy, relaxed.

But why am I asleep? The last thing I remember, it was just after school.

A thread of panic weaves itself into my consciousness. Why can't I recall anything after school ended?

It takes more effort than it should to open my eyes, and when I do, I close them again, convinced I must still be dreaming.

I'm lying on a bed, but I'm not in my room. I'm not even in my house. Still, this place is familiar. I've been here before. Most of the space is dominated by the queen-size mattress I'm lying on. The bifold closet doors are cracked open, and some wadded-up T-shirts are escaping through the gap at the bottom. A bedside table to my right is streaked with dust in a way that suggests whatever was on it was hastily swept away to give the appearance of cleanliness.

I sit up. This is Fox's bedroom. Why on earth am I here? Why don't I remember arriving? And even if I do have a perfectly valid reason for being at Fox's house, it doesn't explain why I'm in his *room*. I quickly take stock of myself. All my clothes are on, which is a relief—or at least as much of one as anything can be, given the rest of the situation.

Before I can figure anything else out, the door swings open to reveal Fox, shirtless and smiling, carrying a plate topped with slices of cold pepperoni pizza and a glass of water.

My first instinct is to ask what I'm doing here, but I fight it. Fox isn't surprised by my presence, and I need to figure out why. How long have I been here? Why did I come?

And why, oh why isn't Fox wearing a shirt?

He settles on the mattress and situates the plate between us. "Okay, now can we continue?"

I stare at him, completely at a loss for what to say. Continue what? Whatever activity led to his current state of undress? Did he spill something on it in the kitchen? Or was he like that before he left this room? The icy weight of dread settles in my stomach. Did I take it off him?

I rub the pads of my thumbs over my fingertips as my eyes trace the lines of his chest and abdomen. Am I imagining things, or do these hands already know what his skin feels like?

Fox releases a soft chuckle. "You're not getting out of this conversation that easily. Do I need to put my shirt back on so you can concentrate?" He takes a sip from the glass before handing it to me. I glance at the table. Does he want me to set the glass down? His eyebrows draw together in confusion. "I thought you said you were thirsty."

I hastily take a few gulps of water. If he got this glass for me, why did he take a sip? That's not something friends do—it's too intimate.

A thought begins forming in the back of my mind, but I don't want to acknowledge it. I think I know what's happening, but—no. I can't accept it.

"Look," he says, his voice soft, "I get that coming clean will have consequences, but I think it's best for everyone involved." A corner of his mouth twitches. "If I'm honest, I can't believe we've kept it secret for this long. I thought for sure Griffin figured it out, but if he hasn't said anything to you, I doubt he has."

My mind is spinning. What could Griffin have to do with this?

"I understand you don't want Dana and Owen to get hurt, but what you don't see is we're already hurting them. The longer we keep this going without telling them, the more it will hurt when they do find out. Dana and I are almost constantly fighting. She wants more from me than I can give her because I don't love her. I love—"

I stand up. I can't hear him say it.

Am I cheating on Owen? How long has this been going on? And how could Fox ever have agreed to this? Does he miss his relationship with the girl I used to be so much he's willing to think I'm the kind of person who would be unfaithful to her boyfriend?

Fox stands, too, his eyebrows drawn together. "Is something wrong?"

I could almost laugh at the question. Is something wrong? No, not something—*everything*. I can't stay here any longer. I have to get away. My agitation grows by the second, and if I don't leave soon, I'm afraid the Influence will make an appearance. If it does, will I simply fall back into Fox's arms—or will it be the darker, more dangerous flavor of the power that takes over? What if I do something to hurt Fox? I don't want to think about it. I can't.

I need to get home. I know I have to tell Fox what's happening to me, but I have no idea how to explain. How long will it take to try? How long until he believes me? What if, in the middle of it, the Influence takes over again? I can't have that. I can't risk staying here.

"I got a text from my parents while you were in the kitchen. They need me home now." It's a lame lie, but it's the best I can come up with.

"Did something happen?"

I start for the door. "I don't know. They just want me home." I hesitate before stepping into the hallway. What if someone else is here? But I dismiss the idea. Who else would be here? Griffin has his own apartment, and their dad is usually on the road for work.

By the time I make it into the hall, Fox is at my heels. "Aren't you going to take your bike?"

I stop in the middle of the living room. Of course I didn't drive her. If I'm here in secret, I wouldn't want my car sitting in the driveway. I cut through the dining room to get to the side door in the kitchen. Sure enough, my bicycle is parked beside the house.

I feel Fox's eyes on me as I mount the bike. "We have to face this sooner or later. Think about it, but know I can't keep lying forever."

Unsure of how to respond, I place my feet on the pedals and start down the driveway.

The tears don't start falling until I'm around the block. What's happening to me? Am I leading a secret life—one even I don't know about? How long has this been going on?

And how will I ever explain this to Owen? I have to, I know that. Fox is at least right on that point. Whatever has been going on between the two of us needs to come to light, but not so Fox and I can be together. Owen needs to know the truth, but the thought of telling him makes my blood run cold. How could he ever forgive me? I don't even know for sure what's been going on with Fox, but it's safe to assume it hasn't been innocent. Owen has been so caring, so understanding—so patient. He hasn't pushed me about anything, even though I'm certain there are things he's wanted to push me on. He's rubbed my back, held my hand, given me a shoulder to lean against. How will he react when he finds out I may have been giving so much more to Fox?

The tears are coming so fast now that I have to stop the bike so I don't crash. How many things will the Influence steal from me before I'm finally rid of it?

Chapter Seventeen
Brody

I hate that I've had to resort to lurking.

I was confident Krissa would have reconsidered and accepted my offer by now. But she hasn't, and it's making me nervous. I can't come back to Jade empty-handed.

That's why, even though I feel like a stalker, I'm sitting in my parked car down the street from Fox Holloway's house. I followed Krissa here over an hour ago. I toyed with the idea of shielding my presence from onlookers and getting closer to the house to see if I could determine what's going on, but prudence keeps me in my seat. If Krissa senses my presence, there's no telling what the Influence will make her do. I saw how angry she was when she caught a glimpse of me on Main the other day, and I wasn't even trying to follow her then.

I bang my hand against the steering wheel. She has all that rage and darkness inside her. How is she content to stay here in her tiny life in Clearwater? From my research, the one constant I have seen in those possessed by the Influence is they love power and control. They're violent to the extreme. The Amaranthine would feed both those desires. She has to know that.

Perhaps she's more interested in feeding desires of another kind. This isn't the first time I've followed her to Fox's house. Publicly, she appears to be with Owen, but something different is going on in private.

There's movement in the Holloways' driveway, then Krissa comes speeding down on her bike. For a moment I'm worried she might notice me, but as she draws near, it's clear she's too upset to notice much of anything. I wait till she passes, then start the engine and follow her as she rounds the corner.

I'm careful to stay behind her. Upset must be an understatement: Even from my angle, I can tell she's wiping away tears.

She travels only about a block before coming to a stop. Her shoulders shake and she covers her face with her hands. Slowly, I pull the car up so I'm even with her. What could have happened to make her behave like this? Did she unwittingly do something to hurt Fox? If that's the case, maybe she's closer to accepting my offer than I thought.

I consider getting out of the car and approaching her, but now is probably not the most opportune time. Maybe I can wait until tomorrow—perhaps even later tonight. I only brought the one picture of Owen, so if I want to cast another summoning spell, I'll need to figure out a different element to put inside the circle.

I'm so preoccupied with making my plans that I don't notice someone approach my car. When knuckles wrap on the window beside me, it's all I can do to keep from jumping. It's Krissa. Her cheeks are tear-stained and her face is red, but her eyes aren't filled with sadness—they're filled with rage. I don't like that look, but I open my door and step out onto the street anyway.

"What, are you stalking me now?" she snaps. "How many times to I have to tell you: I'm not interested in your offer. You might as well leave town. Stop skulking around, watching me, like some sort of pervert."

I try not to let it show on my face that my actions have left me feeling like exactly the kind of person she's describing. But I've been waiting for an opportunity like this for days. I've run through a scenario like this dozens of times in my mind, and I know exactly what to say. "You're not interested in the least? Forgive me if I don't believe you. Why do you insist on pretending you're a normal person with a normal life? What's inside you is extraordinary. Instead of fighting it, why not use it?"

Her eyes narrow. "You want me to use it?" Her voice is a low growl. Something in her eyes shifts. The anger from moments ago disappears, replaced by a kind of vacant glassiness that chills me to my core. Her lip curls like an animal's snarl.

Something's not right. This isn't a deeper level of anger; it's something different, something far darker. I pass my hand from side to side in front of her face, but her gaze doesn't follow it. It's like she can't even see me anymore. I need to get away from her. I'm not the kind of person whose fight-or-flight reflex often leans toward the latter option, but now I know it's my only chance. I reach behind me for the door handle, but before my fingers gain purchase, her hand darts forward, covering my chest. She curls her fingers, digging her nails through my shirt and into my flesh.

She's going to rip out my heart. I don't know why the wild thought flies into my mind, but once it's there, I can't deny its veracity. There's no doubt in my mind the Influence has taken her over and she means to kill me. I need to move, fight back, do something—but I'm frozen. She's cast some kind of spell over me that keeps me from getting away from her.

My skin stings as her nails break it. For someone so small, she's incredibly strong. But the strength isn't coming from her, of course—this is all the Influence.

Pressure continues to build on the spot over my heart. I've never given much thought to how I'll die, but even if I had, this scenario never would have occurred to me. To have my heart ripped out by someone so young, a near novice in the ways of magic, would have been unthinkable. But this is no ordinary girl, and this is no ordinary magic.

I can't move my head to look down, but I'm positive her

fingertips have burrowed their way into my chest. The pain is worse than anything I've ever experienced. Maybe I'll be lucky and pass out from the pain before she manages to get to my heart.

Then Krissa pulls her hand away and takes a step back, gasping like she's coming up for breath after being submerged in water. When her eyes raise to meet mine, the glassy expression is gone, replaced by a terror so complete it almost affects me. "If you value your life, you should go now," she says, her voice quiet.

I don't need to be told twice. Finally able to control my body again, I open my car door and slide behind the passenger seat. I don't bother to put the seatbelt on before I peel off down the street, desperate to get some space between her and me.

She's more unpredictable than I imagined she would be, but at least I'm starting to understand why: She's fighting it. I suppose it makes sense, in a way. In all the other accounts I've found, people under Influence willingly allowed it to inhabit them. Krissa may have let it in, but only to keep it out of her friends. It was never her intention to use it.

I'm actually relieved she's fighting it—if she weren't, I'd be dead right now.

It's possible I've miscalculated. Maybe Krissa isn't the right fit to become our assassin. But how can I go back and tell that to Jade? If I fail, Lena will no doubt be right there, pushing her list of potential candidates. If that happens, there's no way I'll ever become high priest.

Krissa has to be the assassin. I just need to figure out how to turn her into one.

Chapter Eighteen
Krissa

My heart finally stops racing by the time I make it home. As I wheel my bike back to the garage, my mind is spinning. What's going on with me? I could have killed Brody. The idea doesn't horrify me nearly as much as it should, and my stomach twists. The Influence is getting stronger every day. What happens the next time it takes over? Will I be able to stop myself before I do something terrible?

I pull my phone from my back pocket and text Owen as I walk toward the house. I need to see him. I know I need to tell him about everything that happened today—not just with Brody, but with Fox—but I'm not sure I can. I'm still not sure how to explain what's been happening with Fox. I don't even have all the details. All I know is Owen is the one who chases the Influence away, and that's exactly what I need right now.

My phone buzzes as I cross the threshold. *I'm caught up with family, but I'll be done soon.*

I sigh with relief. *Good. Come over as soon as you can.*

I close the back door with a little more force than is strictly necessary, and my mom, who happens to be entering the hall at the same moment, clutches at her chest.

"Krissa! I wasn't expecting you home for dinner. I thought you and Bria would be studying for your finals for at least another hour?" She tilts her head and scrutinizes me as I walk toward her. "Are you okay? You look a little... upset."

I shake my head. "It's nothing." It's the lie of the century, but what am I supposed to do? Tell her the truth? There's no way she would be able to handle it. It's kind of an unwritten rule that we don't tell Mom any more than we have to. Lately, I get the sense Jodi is keeping things from my dad, too. I don't blame her, exactly. My parents are getting a second chance at their marriage after five years apart. Hell, they're even planning to renew their vows this summer. They're walking around in a kind of honeymoon daze half the time. I don't want to be the one to kill that buzz. I need to be reminded there's still good in the world, and I think Jodi gets that.

Mom is still watching me, so I force a smile. "We got a little burned out on studying, so we decided to call it quits early instead of goofing off for another hour. I thought you'd like having me home for dinner."

She finally stops searching my face. "Of course I do. You're just in time. It's almost done."

I nod and brush past her. I poke my head into the dining room, but the table is already set. I double back to the kitchen and get another place setting for myself. On my way back, Jodi enters the room.

"Hey, stranger. You're in luck: It's taco night." She hitches her thumb toward the kitchen. "Your dad made enough to feed the whole neighborhood. It's too bad you didn't invite Bria over."

My stomach clenches and I watch her closely. Does Jodi suspect something? Is she saying that because she knows I wasn't with Bria? No, that can't be. Until half an hour ago, even I didn't know the big secret I've been keeping from everyone. If the Influence has been that good at keeping the truth from me, I have to believe it's been able to keep it from everyone else.

At least, I hope that's the case.

I'm spared having to think of a response when Mom and Dad enter the room, carrying bowls filled with various taco toppings. Jodi and I head to the kitchen for more dishes.

I'm glad when Dad doesn't express surprise at my presence. I'm not interested in lying anymore today. As we began filling our plates, Jodi strikes up small talk, asking Mom and Dad about their days at work. I keep my head down, mechanically chewing bite after bite of food that I don't taste.

My phone buzzes in my back pocket, and I take it out. Keeping it under the table, I read the text from Owen. *You're at home, right? Is that where you want to meet?*

"How are the applications going?" Dad's voice is louder than strictly necessary, and I get the feeling he asked the question once already.

I glance up. "Good."

Once my attention is back on my phone, Dad continues, "Have you submitted any yet? Do you need checks for application fees?"

I tap out a response quickly. *Yes, my place.* "Um, no." I'm sure Dad wants more details, but I really don't have anything further to say on the topic.

Dad rests his elbows on the table and steeples his fingers. "Krissa," he says in a tone I remember well from childhood. He always used this voice when I'd been caught doing something wrong—sneaking candy after I'd been told no or throwing a toy when I knew it wasn't allowed. "We're talking about your future here, and you're, what? Texting?"

My phone vibrates again and I can't fight the urge to check Owen's response. *I'm on my way.*

He clears his throat. "I understand you have a lot going on right now, but that's no excuse to ignore me."

The skin on the back of my neck prickles. What part of my complete disinterest in this topic does he not understand? I've shown zero engagement in any of his college talk so far, yet he keeps bringing it up. Right now, the last thing on my mind is higher education. I need Owen, and that's all.

"You understand what's going on with me? You have no idea," I growl, my voice low. Dad's eyes flash with surprise, but I don't give him the opportunity to respond. "You keep talking about college, my future. What don't you realize is, right now, that future doesn't exist for me."

Dad shakes his head in the way adults do when they think a kid is being unreasonable because they don't know the ways of the world. "I know you think that, but you can't live your life in fear. You have to believe we're going to get through this."

I can't believe what I'm hearing. What's this talk about *we*? He doesn't have this darkness inside him. If Jodi and Anya can't figure out a way to get it out of me, his life won't change. He and Mom will still renew their vows; they'll go on a honeymoon. They're young enough that they could even have a new daughter to replace the one who got taken by the darkness. Tendrils of red curl in my periphery. "Since you came back, you've been pretending like you know everything—but guess what? You don't have a clue what you're talking about."

Jodi shifts and stretches a hand toward my dad. "Ben, maybe we ought to let the subject drop for now. College is still at least a year away. There's plenty of time to make these decisions."

Dad bangs a hand on the tabletop. "I don't need you taking her side, Jodi."

She shakes her head. "I'm not taking sides. I just think everyone needs to step back and calm down."

Dad bangs his hand again. "Calm? I am calm!"

Mom reaches over and rests a hand on his shoulder. "Honey…"

He shakes off her hand. Heat burns in my belly. The red swirls nearer to the center of my vision. Who does he think he is? He left with little explanation five years ago, and when he returned, he expected to seamlessly step back into the role of father. But he hasn't earned it. He gave it up when he left, and it's not his to take back now. "This is all your fault—everything. You say you knew what you were doing when you left, but you never told us. You claim you left to defeat Seth, but you didn't, did you? That was me. I defeated him. And when Crystal needed to be saved, that was me, too. You have done nothing to protect me. I can take care of myself. I don't need you—especially not when you're trying to pretend like everything's fine." A crackle of electricity shoots through my arms and down into my fingertips. Heat surges in my body as the Influence rises up. I try to push it back, but it's so strong. Stronger even than it was with Brody earlier today. "If you know what's good for you, you'll leave me alone and let me handle things my own way."

Dad stares at me with wide eyes. His hands press into the armrests of his chair, and his fingers curl around the edges like he's afraid he'll be swept away in the wave of my anger. "I'm sorry, honey. You're right. I won't talk about college anymore. Why don't you sit down?"

I look down. When did I stand up? Dad's right—I should sit. But no matter how hard I try, I can't make my body comply. The red darkens, blotting out much of my vision. I can only see what's directly in front of me now.

"Just sit down, honey," he says quietly.

How dare he try to order me around? He keeps talking, repeating things like "calm down," "relax," and "sit down," but the sounds blend together into white noise. He can't tell me what to do. He doesn't know better than me. He claims he left me to keep me safe, but all he did was leave me vulnerable. Why didn't he ever tell me about Seth? If he'd done that, I would have known better than to go back in time to get the crystal—I never would've released him in the first place. Everything would be different if he'd simply told me the truth. Everything that's gone wrong is his fault.

He stands and stretches his hand out to me, but as soon as he's on his feet, he's being pressed backward into the wall. My hand rises in front of me and my fingers curl like claws. At the same moment, Dad grabs at his throat. He wheezes and gasps. But he can't draw breath.

Shrill, high voices fill my ears. Mom and Jodi are crying out. They want me to stop. But I can't.

I don't want to.

Dad's face is red and his eyes bulge. My vision is almost completely blocked out now, but before the Influence takes over completely, someone grips me by the shoulders and spins me around. Rage rises within me and I prepare to strike out at whoever is daring to interrupt me, but then I catch a glimpse of clear blue eyes. Owen's gaze locks on me and in a flash, I remember who I am. The burning heat in my body turns itself down to a gentle simmer as Owen wraps me in his arms and pulls me toward the ground.

"Come back to me, Krissa. Come back to me," he murmurs in my ear as we settle on the floor. He repeats the words over and over, his voice filling my ears, clearing my head.

By degrees, the crackling in my veins dies down and the Influence's hold on me ebbs. I clutch Owen for dear life. What would have happened if he hadn't shown up? I've never felt the Influence so strong. Would this have been the time it took over for good? Once my conscious mind was completely overwhelmed, would it have killed my father?

"Dad." I breathe his name like a prayer. I struggle to get to my feet, only managing with Owen's help.

My father sits slumped in the dining room chair. My mom crouches in front of him, her fingers feathering touches over his neck as she examines his face.

Tears sting my eyes. "I'm so sorry," I whisper. "I never meant to hurt you, Dad."

He glances up, but only for a moment, like he can't bear to look at me. I'm sure he'd like to tell me he accepts my apology, that it's okay, but we both know it's not.

I turn to Owen and he wraps his arms around my waist. "What did I do?"

He shakes his head resolutely. "It wasn't you."

I know that's not the truth. "I choked my own dad, Owen. He could've died and it would've been my fault. We have to do something."

"It's okay," he murmurs. "We'll figure out a way to control it."

A humorless laugh escapes my lips. "Control. I think I lost the ability to control it a while ago. I just didn't want to admit it. I didn't want to admit it, and I almost killed my father because of that." I blink, and tears drip down my cheeks. "We have to get the Influence out." I tear my gaze from Owen's face and scan the room until my eyes land on Jodi. "You have to kill me."

Chapter Nineteen
Fox

I'm still not sure exactly what happened with Krissa. She was fine when I left the room for snacks. I was only gone two minutes, and she said she was fine, but clearly there was more going on than she let on.

She's obviously against the idea of coming clean about our relationship, but I can't wrap my head around why. I get that she doesn't want to hurt anyone, but sometimes it's inevitable.

I take a bite of cold pizza before setting the slice back down in the box and getting back to picking up around the house. Dad will be home tomorrow, and I'm really not interested in sitting through another lecture about what a slob I am. At least when Griffin was living here, he could shoulder some of the blame. Although, if I'm honest, the house has been messier these last several months since the circle stopped meeting regularly. We always met in the basement, but I still made sure the upstairs didn't get too out of hand. Now I only clean up when I know Dad or Dana is coming over. Krissa usually doesn't spend enough time in the main part of the house to mind whether or not things are organized.

I'm sorting through a stack of mail when the doorknob twists. I freeze, my mind spinning. Did I get the date wrong? Is Dad due home today? Or is it Krissa, returning to explain about her freak earlier?

Envelopes still in hand, I step out of the dining room and into the living room as the front door swings open. Griffin crosses the threshold and offers a half smile when he sees me.

"Hey," I say, confused. I can count on one hand how many times he's been back here since he moved out, and now he's dropping by a second time in just over a week? "Is it laundry day again already?"

Griffin closes the door behind him. "Can't a guy stop by to see his little brother?"

I snort. I know him well enough to be certain he has a reason for the visit, and that it has nothing to do with being sentimental.

"Sorry to interrupt your Martha Stewart moment," he says, nodding toward the paper in my hand. He steps into the dining room and swipes a piece of pizza out of the open box. "Dad coming home soon?"

I lay the mail down and begin separating it into two piles—one for bills and the other for junk. "Yeah, he is. But I doubt that's why you're here." Taking advantage of his mouthful of food, I add, "You should stop by when he's home. Despite what you think, he'd like to see you." I've done my best to stay out of my brother's relationship with our dad, but that doesn't mean I like things the way they are. When I was growing up, I was always jealous of how close the two of them were. Griffin loved going out to the garage and learning about how engines worked. I preferred staying inside and drawing in my sketchbook. Dad said I inherited the itch to sketch from my mom. He claimed I took after her, while Griffin was more like him. But after the elder council spell revealed to Dad that Griffin and I both possessed magic like our mom, it was like it was the only thing he could see anymore. Despite the fact that he only spends a few days home each month, he banned us from using magic in the house. Griffin couldn't live with it, so he moved out.

Griffin waves away my suggestion before shoving the rest of his slice into his mouth and picking up a couple of empty Chinese food cartons. He stuffs them into a stray grocery bag he finds under the table. "So, saw your girlfriend today."

The back of my neck prickles. Is this why he stopped by? I say nothing, waiting to see where he's going.

"She brought her aunt's car in for an oil change." He picks up a few receipts and glances at them before adding them to the bag. "I was actually on my way out, but she saw me and struck up a conversation. So I asked her how Italian night went."

I freeze. I let him assume I was making dinner for Dana the other night—how could I not? I wasn't prepared to get caught in a lie.

"It was funny," he continues. "She had no idea what I was talking about."

My brain scrambles for an explanation. "I burned the food," I say quickly. "I was too embarrassed to tell her about how epically I failed, so I ordered something before she got here."

Griffin narrows his eyes, studying me shrewdly. "You're on dangerous ground, little brother. If you don't want to be with Dana, cut her loose. She doesn't deserve to be lied to."

My heart thuds in my chest. He knows. But how much does he know? If he had an inkling Krissa was the other girl in the equation, we'd be having a very different conversation right now. The two of them never hit it off in all the time I was dating her, but something changed this winter and they became friends. Griffin may be a dick, but he's loyal, and when he decides to count someone as a friend, it's for life.

I feel his eyes on me. "You have no idea what you're talking about." I keep my focus on the task of sorting mail, but my movements are mechanical. I'm not sure I'm putting things in the right spots anymore.

"Maybe. For your sake—and Dana's—I hope I don't." He picks up another slice of pizza and pivots on his heel. "Let me know when you find out how long Dad's staying in town. Maybe I'll drop by."

As soon as the front door closes behind him, I sink into a dining room chair and inhale deeply. Will Griffin keep digging until he knows the truth? Will he tell Dana what he suspects? Or is Dana already suspicious after his question?

This is it—the final straw. I don't care if Krissa doesn't like it. We have to come clean, because if we don't, the truth will find its way out anyway, and the people she's hoping to protect will be hurt worse than she can imagine. The next time I can get her alone, I'll make her see that.

Chapter Twenty
Krissa

I lie on my bed, staring out the windows on my right. The sky is bright blue—exactly the shade of Owen's eyes. I imagine the color seeping into me and filling up all the spaces in my body. If I can hold on to the color—the feeling—maybe everything will turn out all right.

Owen tightens his arm around my abdomen. There's been a moratorium on the no-boys-in-the-bedroom rule, and he and I have spent most of the day snuggled beside each other just like this. Jodi lifted the ban after my parents left for work. She told me she figured she didn't need to worry about what the two of us might get up to unsupervised since she and Anya are downstairs. Besides, with what's going to happen today, my thoughts couldn't be further from romance.

"Are you sure you want to do this?" he murmurs, his lips close to my ear.

I squeeze his hands. "No matter how many times you ask me, the answer's going to be yes."

He takes in a breath. "I don't like this at all. Are you sure there's no other way?"

It's not the first time he's asked this question, either. I roll over to face him and settle a hand on his cheek. "I know it's dangerous, but it's the only way. I can't risk hurting someone again. You were there—you saw it. I could've killed my dad last night. If this spell will finally get the Influence out of me, it'll be worth it."

"And what if it doesn't? What if something goes wrong?" He covers my hand with his. "I can't lose you."

My eyes sting, and I close them against the tears threatening to build. I can't say the same fear hasn't plagued me since I suggested this last night. But I can't risk losing control again. I outright refused to go to school today, terrified something might set me off and Owen wouldn't be around to keep the Influence from taking over completely.

Keeping my eyes shut, I lean forward until my lips find Owen's. I don't want to lose him, either. "I love you," I murmur against his mouth. I hadn't wanted to say it before, afraid for so many reasons it wasn't the right time—but now I'm afraid I won't have the chance again. Before I go through with this spell, I need him to know.

He pulls away and my heart clenches. Panic floods me. I shouldn't have said it. Telling him was selfish. Now things are going to be awkward.

When he doesn't speak, I open my eyes, ready to apologize, but the intensity of his gaze stills my tongue.

"I love you, too."

And then we're kissing again, although I'm not sure which of us initiated. My leg wraps around his and he pulls me tight against him. My cheeks are damp, and I'm not sure whether I'm crying or he is. Maybe we both are.

As Owen holds me, I find I'm no longer scared. It's not that I'm suddenly convinced everything will work out, because I'm not. There's a very real possibility I won't make it through the spell. I'm simply able to lose myself in this moment, in the feel of Owen's body, in the taste of our saltwater kisses, in the completeness of his love.

***

Owen and I sit, hands linked, on the living room couch as Jodi explains the spell to the assembled witches and psychics. It's the same crowd as last time, but there's a distinctly nervous energy that wasn't present before. Lexie and Bria pale visibly as Jodi finishes talking. Griffin rubs the back of his neck nervously. Crystal and Dana stare resolutely at the floor. Even the adults—Anya, Shelly, and David—look a little ill.

I don't blame them. When they showed up today, I don't think anyone expected this to be the reason. I can't imagine what's going through their minds right now.

I haven't been able to bring myself to glance in Fox's direction. If I look at him, I won't be able to stop wondering what's going on in his mind, and I can't let myself be distracted right now.

After a few moments of heavy silence, Jodi glances at me and nods. When we discussed going through with this spell last night, I made it clear I wanted to address everyone beforehand. I shift in my seat, and Owen squeezes my fingers as I begin speaking. "To be clear, what we're asking you to do is dangerous. In case you were wondering, this is dark magic. Anyone who doesn't want to be a part of this can stand down—no questions asked. I won't think you're betraying me. None of you owe me this." My vision begins to swim. I try my hardest not to blink, but it doesn't work, and the tears stream down my face. "I don't want to make any of you do something you don't want to."

No one speaks, but it's not like I expect them to. This isn't like any spell we've done before. I wasn't kidding last night when I told Jodi she had to kill me. We're here today to stop my heart in the hope that the Influence will sense I'm no longer a suitable host and leave my body. There are more dangers involved than I care to think about, but I'm willing to go through with it if it means I won't hurt anyone ever again.

Bridget raises her hand timidly, like a shy girl in a classroom. "Can I ask... What's the danger? I mean, obviously I see the risk for you, Krissa, but what's the danger for the rest of us?"

Anya takes a step forward. "Nothing direct. In fact, there's every likelihood we can cast the spell without any negative effects on us. The danger of dark magic is far more subtle. It's a seductive force. Having that kind of power over people can be addicting. The more magic is used for darkness, the harder it is to stop using it that way."

Bridget twists her hands in her lap and stares at a spot on the floor. "I'm probably not alone in this, but when I was bound to the crystal, I used magic the wrong way." She glances at Dana for a fleeting moment, and I'm reminded of how she used a love spell to steal the affections of Dana's then-boyfriend. She hurt Dana physically, too—first by causing her to trip and nearly break her nose, then by knocking her down a flight of stairs, resulting in a broken leg. "I've already been touched by darkness."

I bite my lower lip, confident of what she'll say next. She won't help for fear of the darkness overwhelming her. I can't say I blame her. I'm not even mad; instead, I hope she doesn't feel too guilty for deciding not to take part in this spell.

Bridget looks up, scanning the room, meeting the eyes of every person here. It's not until her gaze lands on mine that she speaks again. "I know the difference between using that kind of power for something bad and for something good. I'm not afraid to use it to help you now."

More tears tumble down my cheeks and Owen slides an arm around my waist as others begin to speak up.

"I'll do it," Lexie says.

"Me, too," Felix says.

Griffin leans forward in his chair. "You know I'm in."

I'm completely overwhelmed as each person in the room agrees to help. I didn't expect this. I expected some—most—to choose not to take the risk. For the first time, confidence fills me. This could work. In fact, I'm starting to believe it will.

Jodi and Anya switch to organizing mode and begin indicating where people should stand and what different roles they will have. I don't pay much attention. Just like last time, my part is easy: all I have to do is lie down.

Bria and West move the coffee table out of the way, and Owen helps me to the floor. I breathe deeply. The ever-present thrum of the Influence builds in my veins. It hasn't been this strong all day. I think it knows what we're about to do. It knows, and it's scared. As Owen takes his place in the circle surrounding me, I close my eyes, allowing the Influence's fear to calm me.

***

My chest burns and my head swims. I gasp. My lungs squeeze the air back out and I take in a new breath of oxygen. I feel like I've been drowning.

The spell is over. The spell is over, and I'm alive. Part of me didn't think I would come back. There was a chance I would have to stay under too long and that even dark magic wouldn't be able to revive me.

But here I am.

All around me is sound and movement, and I struggle to focus on what's happening. It's taking some time for my brain to properly process the input it's receiving. Owen kneels beside me, and when I reach for him, he helps me sit up. His fingertips brush loose strands of hair behind my ears as his eyes search my face.

"Are you all right?"

I reach up and catch his hands in mine. I want to tell him I'm fine, that our gamble worked and the Influence is gone, but before I can form the words, I know it's a lie. As my mind begins processing language again, I become aware of sensations in my body. The Influence is still there, but it's different from before. Stronger. It's not just the burning feeling or the ripple of electricity anymore—

now there's a thrum of emotions attached. The Influence is angry. It knows these people tried to kill me, its host, and it wants to strike out against them before they have a chance to do it again. It doesn't want to give me up.

Heat flows into my fingers and they begin to itch with the desire to cast spells. It takes all my energy not to give in.

"We ended it too soon," Jodi murmurs, standing close to Anya, Shelly, David, and Elliot. "If we waited for even thirty more seconds to bring her back..."

"Do you even hear yourself right now?" Elliot asks, his voice just as low. "We kept her under as long as was safe. Any longer and she might not have come back at all."

Anya casts a furtive glance in my direction. "Should we try again?"

Elliot's eyebrows hike up his forehead. "Are you insane?" He glances at Jodi and shakes his head. "You are. You're both insane. I know you want to get this out of her, but there has to be another way."

"What if there's not?" Jodi asks, her voice cracking.

I can't be in this room anymore. With every passing moment, the desire to strike out grows. I don't want to hurt anyone, but the Influence does. If they try to put me under again, I don't know what will happen, but I can only assume it won't be good.

I shift, intending to stand, but I can't quite get my feet under me. Owen wraps his strong arms around me and helps me up. All noise in the room dissipates, leaving an uncomfortable silence. "I need to go to my room. I'm weak." It's only partially true. I'll allow them to think the spell took a toll because I don't want to see the shame or fear in their eyes that will surely come from me telling them I'm using all my energy to keep the Influence at bay. "We'll find another way. It's okay. Thank you for trying."

Felix, Lexie, and Griffin all take steps toward me like they want to give me a hug or reassure me in some way, but I shake my head and ask Owen to help me to my room.

After he helps me onto my bad, he sits beside me and traces a finger down my cheek. "Are you sure you're okay? Can I bring you something? I could have Jodi make a tea."

I shake my head. "I'm fine. I just need to rest."

His eyebrows furrow as he studies me, and for a moment, I'm afraid he can somehow pick up on my lie. I'm not fine—I'm possibly the farthest thing from it. And as much as I want him here with me, I need at least a little time to myself. I know he won't approve of what I'm about to do.

After a long moment, he finally says, "Okay."

He moves to stand, but I brush his arm with my fingertips. "Could you hand me my phone?" When he raises an eyebrow, I come up with a plausible reason for needing it. "I want to set an alarm so I don't sleep too long."

After another pause, he does as I ask. He turns away like he's ready to leave the room, but then he spins around and leans down to press a kiss to my lips. My hands find the back of his neck and I pull him down to me. I kiss him fiercely, as if doing so can provide me the strength I need for what I have to do next.

When we finally separate, he takes a step away from my bed. "If I don't leave now, I won't be able to." The look in his eyes makes it clear he doesn't want to go, but he knows it's what's best for me right now. "You should nap. We can pick this up when you're feeling better."

I nod and Owen waves before starting for the stairs. I wait until his footsteps fade before unlocking my phone and opening the messaging app. I tap on Sasha's name before typing out a message.

I'm ready to do the dissevering spell.

Chapter Twenty-One
Brody

"I was under the impression you would be back already, new assassin in hand."

I do my best to keep my expression neutral. Apparently dissatisfied with my written reports, Jade decided to check in with me today via video call. She's mentioned to me before that her main reason for choosing this method is to read a person's face as he talks, in order to gauge whether or not he's lying. I wonder if she remembers telling me that.

I weigh my response carefully. Pointing out that I never gave her a specific amount of time I expected this mission to take doesn't seem like my best move. I don't want to tell her she's wrong to her face and sound insolent—or worse, petulant. "I have the situation well in hand."

Jade's eyebrows raise. "Really? If that were the case, I would assume she'd have accepted your offer already. Or are you telling me she has, and you're simply staying in town for the nightlife?"

I can't help snorting at the idea of Clearwater having any sort of nightlife I might find entertaining. Could Jade honestly think I'd find drinking domestic beers down by the river or watching a movie at the bookstore at all engaging? "I'll admit, things aren't progressing as quickly as I originally anticipated. The Influence is making Krissa a bit more unpredictable than I imagined."

"Perhaps she isn't the right fit," says another voice from off-screen. My muscles tense as I place its owner. Before she speaks again, Lena appears over Jade's shoulder. "We don't want an assassin we can't control."

I inhale deeply through my nose. What is Lena doing in Jade's office? Did Jade invite her to sit in on this call? If so, it seems Lena has been able to get into the high priestess's good graces faster than I would have thought possible. It took me years to become a member of her inner circle.

Only a slight flicker of irritation on Jade's face gives me hope that Lena's presence isn't entirely welcome.

"Krissa is fighting the Influence," I say, hoping to turn the conversation's focus back to me. "I've seen it firsthand." My free hand rubs my chest. Even though I was able to heal the damage caused by her fingernails, a ghost of pain remains in the spot just above my heart. "I'm fairly certain that's the problem. She's unpredictable because the Influence wants to do things that aren't in line with her will."

Lena makes a show of rolling her eyes before shoving a piece of paper between Jade and the screen. "I have a list of candidates I'm confident will be pliable to our will and purposes. We don't need to try to convince someone who's unpredictable and has no reason to give us her loyalty."

Besides the paper, only Jade's eyes are visible on the screen. They flick down at whatever is written on the list before her hand edges it out of the way. "I'm not exactly overwhelmed by any of these names. Judging by the reputations of at least half of them, I doubt they'd be aligned with our mission, either. I don't even recognize at least a quarter of them. Where did you find these candidates?"

I do my best to keep a satisfied smirk off my face. Lena hasn't impressed Jade—I still have a chance. "I have no doubt Krissa will be entirely controllable once she stops fighting the Influence." It's an outright lie: I have no idea whether Krissa will be more or less pliable once she gives in to the Influence. But it's the only card I have to play.

Jade glances down, I assume at the list again, before staring back into the screen. "You have one week. If you can't get Krissa to accept your offer by then, I'll be forced to go in another direction. Do you understand?"

I can't help feeling her words carry more weight than what is obvious on the surface. If I don't come through, there's little doubt in my mind she won't endorse me to be her successor. "I understand."

She nods. "Good. In the meantime, Lena, I want you to get back to work on the other problem in Crystal Taylor's message. We still have no idea what the 'power of deepest night' is. I want everything in order so once we have an assassin, nothing will stand in our way from acquiring the carcinite and our immortality."

Lena ducks her head, and I fight another smile. Jade is giving me another chance. I won't let her down. I can't. My future depends on it.

Chapter Twenty-Two
Fox

I haven't been able to talk to Krissa since she left my house so abruptly the other day. She hasn't been at school and hasn't responded to any of my text messages. I didn't even have a chance to get her alone at her house last night before or after the spell. I'm so worried about her. It's killing me that she won't even let me check in. If she's still mad about me wanting to tell everyone the truth about us, I wish she'd tell me. All this avoidance is making me crazy.

I stand outside the shop two doors down from Hannah's Herbs. There was a time when I knew Krissa's work schedule backward and forward, but it's been so erratic lately I don't know if she's even working regular hours anymore.

I should walk in and see if she's there. It's not outside the realm of the ordinary for me to shop there. Simply going in won't reveal our secret.

I'm not sure what keeps me from doing it. How will she react if she is there? Will she talk to me, or will she go hide in the back room until I leave? I hate that she's mad at me and there's nothing I can do to fix it. I hate that she's not giving me the opportunity to fix things.

I glance toward Hannah's Herbs. I haven't seen anyone come in or out in the five minutes I've been standing here. It's entirely possible there are no customers inside. Now might be my best opportunity to talk with her alone—provided she's working.

Before I start toward the store, I glance down Main Street in the opposite direction to make sure no one I recognize is out and about. The last thing I want is someone we know to walk in while we're talking. My scan doesn't turn up anyone heading toward the shop, but a familiar form steps onto the sidewalk from near the bookstore, making my trip inside unnecessary.

Krissa hasn't caught sight of me yet. Her gaze is fixed on the pavement in front of her. I jog toward her.

She's distracted, consulting a piece of paper, and she doesn't notice me until I'm an arm's length away. The look on her face indicates she's less than pleased to see me. She glances nervously down the street beyond me as she hastily tucks the paper into her back pocket. "Hello."

The formality in her tone hits me like a punch. It couldn't be clearer that I'm the last person she wants to be running into. "You haven't responded to any of my messages. You've been ignoring me at school. We need to talk."

She shakes her head and attempts to walk past me. "Now is not a good time."

I grab the crook of her arm with my hand and she reluctantly turns to face me. "Too bad. Look, I'm sorry if I pushed too hard the other night, it's just... I'm tired of living like this. I'm sick of lying to everyone. I'm trying to understand where you're coming from, but the more I think about it, the more I disagree. Keeping this a secret—keeping us a secret—we can't do it anymore."

She's shaking her head again. "I really can't talk about this right now."

"I get that this isn't an ideal venue." While I don't recognize anyone, it doesn't change the fact that there are dozens of people walking up and down Main. "My truck's down the street. Let's go for a drive and—"

She takes a step back. "No. I can't."

"Yes, you can." It occurs to me that I may have caught her on a break from working at the shop, so I add, "Just for a little while."

She can't hold my gaze. "I'm meeting Owen."

My stomach clenches. He was already at her house when I arrived for the spell last night. I saw them come downstairs from her room, and it took everything in me to suppress the wave of jealousy. I should have been the one comforting her beforehand, not him. The fact that she wants to blow me off so she can go see him now is almost more than I can take.

She rubs her bare arms as if trying to ward off a chill. "But you're right about one thing—we can't keep lying."

A bubble of hope builds in my chest. Maybe this is what's kept her from responding for the last couple of days—she's been sorting out how to end things with Owen. "I'm so glad you agree. I'll let you go so you can break up with Owen, and I'll go and tell Dana. Then—"

"No."

I stare, sure I've heard her incorrectly. "But you just said..."

Her gaze dips for a moment before fixing on my face again. "I'm not breaking up with Owen. It's you I need to end things with, Fox."

I squeeze my eyes closed and open them again, sure I've slipped into some sort of weird nightmare. But Krissa is still looking at me with the same sad gaze. "What are you talking about? Are you mad that I'm making you choose? I'm sorry if you think I'm pushing you, but—"

She's not paying attention to me anymore. Her attention wanders across the street and her posture goes rigid like she's ready to fight. I follow her gaze, wondering if she's caught sight of Owen, but I don't notice anything out of the ordinary—just a woman in her seventies sitting on a bench.

Krissa tears her gaze away from whatever is holding her attention and reaches forward to squeeze my arm. "I never meant to hurt you. Please believe that. But whatever we had, it's over."

I'm too dumbfounded to respond. All I can do is watch as she crosses the street, leaving me utterly bewildered in her absence.

Chapter Twenty-Three
Brody

I'm at my regular table at the diner, just finishing my meal, when I feel it—the irresistible tug of a summoning spell. I smile as I throw a few bills on the table and head for my car.

Krissa is calling me.

I get behind the wheel and start my engine. I'm not entirely sure where to go, but I don't need to be: the spell will guide me.

As I drive through the streets of Clearwater, I wonder what changed. Earlier this afternoon, I caught a glimpse of her having a rather intense conversation with Fox Holloway on the street. Did something about their exchange make her see reason? Has she finally realized she's not doing herself any favors by holding out hope for a so-called normal life?

I continue driving past some familiar landmarks—a dilapidated farmhouse that was never demolished after a fire; an old red barn with a caved-in roof. Before I even arrive, I know she's summoned me to the same place we met when I first arrived in town.

When she comes into view, I try to read her posture. She stands with her arms crossed over her chest and her eyes narrowed. I can't tell whether she's upset or whether this is the Influence I'm dealing with. Either way, it's not as if I can take my time approaching her. As soon as I'm near enough, I pull the car onto the shoulder and get out. I'm not able to stop moving until I'm safely in the center of the chalk circle.

She glowers, but I keep my face impassive. "You wanted to see me?"

She continues staring for a long moment before speaking. "You need to leave town."

My stomach sinks. "I'll be happy to leave if you'll come with me," I say, flashing a grin I hope doesn't look too forced.

She begins pacing, shaking her head as she walks. "No, you don't understand. You have to leave or I can't be held accountable for what I might do to you."

I'm not the kind of person who scares easily, but at this moment, I can't deny the prickle of fear dancing along my spine.

"We did a spell last night," she says, her voice low. I'm not sure whether she means for me to hear her or not. "I thought it would work. I thought they'd be able to get the Influence out of me, but they couldn't. And now it's even stronger than before. I can't push it down like before. It's taking almost all my concentration to keep it from taking over—and that's when I'm in a good mood. When I'm angry, it's even harder to keep it locked away." She stops pacing and stares at me. "Your presence—your lurking—makes me angry. I saw you on Main earlier today. I bet you thought that stupid glamor would work, but I knew it was you and not an old lady."

I swallow. Not many people are able to see through glamors. Even I can't do it, and there aren't many magical feats I'm incapable of. The Influence must be growing stronger, as she claims.

The fact doesn't comfort me. What happens if it takes over against her will? According to my research, Influence typically complements an individual's personality; I don't know what it would be like to deal with the Influence itself.

I don't want to give her any reason to be more agitated than she already is, but I need to make the most of this opportunity. "You keep trying to fight what's inside you, but I can show you a better way to handle it. I bet you spend most of your day trying your best not to do something to hurt one of your friends or family members. If you try to keep it bottled up for too long, it's bound to come out at the worst moments. But if you come with me, I can give you the outlet you need."

There's a flicker in her eyes—something like desire—but she blinks and it's gone. "I don't want the life you're offering. Why would I want to be an assassin? I don't want to be pointed like a gun at anyone who crosses the Amaranthine. I don't want to live that way. I want a normal life."

I snort. "Why? What's so desirable about that?" I hold up my hands to gesture at our surroundings. "Can you honestly tell me you want to live out your days in this pitiful excuse for a town? Will you really be happy taking over the shop when Jodi tires of running it, pretending to care about the ailments of hypochondriacal customers?" I study her face, but her expression gives nothing away. "Sounds dreadfully boring, if you ask me. I can offer you so much more. The Amaranthine are more powerful than you can imagine. Our business takes us all over the world, to the most exquisite places you could ever dream of."

She squeezes her eyes closed for a beat before responding. "I don't want to be shackled to a group who only wants to use the worst part of me. With the Influence in me—even without it—I know I'm capable of killing. But that's not who I want to be."

I raise my eyebrows. "You'd rather be shackled to one of your boyfriends instead? What kind of life can either of those boys give you?"

She brings her hands together and wrings them. "I don't have... Fox isn't my boyfriend."

I smile. "It doesn't appear that way to me."

She squeezes her hand so hard I'm afraid she may crush her own bones, but at the last second, she drops her arms to her sides. "I don't care what you think you can offer me. I want—I deserve—a happy ending. I'll never stop fighting for it."

She takes a step forward and I will myself not to step back. But instead of reaching for me, she rubs the outer ring of the chalk circle with the tip of her shoe until a section disappears. She's broken the enchantment, and I'm free. "If you know what's good for you, you'll leave. Don't say I haven't warned you."

I don't stick around to continue our conversation. At this point, I'm positive nothing I say will get through to her. I have to try a different plan of attack.

She wants a happy ending, does she? Maybe what she really needs is to see there's no such thing. If I take the possibility of that ending away from her, she'll have no choice but to join me.

Chapter Twenty-Four
Fox

Dana hums happily in the passenger seat of my truck, causing the knot in my stomach to tighten with each turn. When I asked if she wanted to come to my house after school, she brightened like it was Christmas morning. Since our disagreement about Krissa last week, we haven't spent much time together. It doesn't take a psychic to know she thinks this is a good sign for our relationship.

She couldn't be more wrong.

I pull into the driveway and sigh with relief when I don't see my dad's truck. He's still in town for the next few days, but he mentioned this morning that he had some things to take care of this afternoon. I'm glad he didn't change his mind or get done with them early. Being alone will make things at least a little easier.

We jump out of the car and Dana rushes around to my side to take my hand. I let her, even though I know it's sending the wrong signal. I don't want to shake her off and be in a fight before this conversation even begins.

She surveys the living room and dining room as we enter the house, then smiles. "Is your dad in town?"

I'm surprised she knows me well enough to make the guess. Then again, we've been together just over six months. Maybe it shouldn't come as such a shock. Despite her faults, she's been a decent girlfriend. At least, she doesn't deserve what's about to happen. "Yeah, he got in the other day."

I lead her to the couch and catch the shadow of a pout as it crosses her face. "Is he going to be gone long?"

I know why she's asking. When I invited her over, I'm sure she imagined a different chain of events unfolding. To say we took a lot of time using the empty house to our benefit after Griffin moved out would be an understatement. In the last month, though, nearly all of our time together has been spent in public. When I extended the invitation today, I'm positive she was under the impression we'd be taking advantage of some alone time in a different room of the house. "I'm not sure," I say honestly. "He's got some errands to run, but I don't know how long they'll take."

Her expertly arched eyebrows draw together. "So, what's going on?"

I rub the palms of my hands against my denim-clad thighs. "We have to talk."

Before I can continue, she nods. "I know we do. Let me start."

I'm surprised by this enough that I don't object. Am I misreading the entire situation? Dana is a psychic, after all. Even if she can't read my thoughts because of the charm I wear, maybe she's sensed things aren't going to work out between us. I ought to give her the space to say what's on her mind. "Okay."

She takes in a breath and squares her shoulders. "I know things have been tense between us, and I get that a lot of it's been my fault. I know I give the illusion of being self-assured, but in a lot of ways I'm not." She offers a small smile before continuing. "And when my boyfriend spends so much of his energy worrying about his ex-girlfriend... I'm sorry, but that makes me jealous." She reaches over and covers my hand with hers. Squeezing it, she continues. "The thing is, I know I don't have any reason to be. I'm sorry. I'm sorry for acting like I don't trust you, because I do. And from now on, I promise not to let it get the best of me anymore."

I stare at her, completely blown away and unable to form a coherent thought. I am a piece of shit. In fact, I am possibly the worst piece of shit of all time. Here she is, feeling guilty for being jealous when she's had every right to be. What have I been thinking? How could I have been so selfish to believe my actions only affected me and Krissa? No matter what Krissa said, no matter how persuasive her arguments, I shouldn't have let things go on like this for so long. I should have been a better person and done this a while ago. "I'm so sorry you've been feeling like that. You don't deserve it. You deserve to be with someone who makes you feel like you're the center of the world. And I haven't been that person. I can't be that person."

Confusion etches a line between her eyebrows. "Yes, you can," she says slowly. "I believe in you."

I slip my hand out from underneath hers and shake my head. There's not going to be an easy way to say this, so I decide to be direct, like I should have been from the start. "Dana, we need to break up."

She stares blankly, her mouth open just a fraction as she processes the words. She must realize she heard me right because her gaze turns icy and she stands, balling her fists. "You're breaking up with me? Out of nowhere? You can't do that."

I stand, too, but not to be confrontational. I simply want to be on her level. I keep my voice low and even. "I can. I just did."

I try to brush a hand down her arm, but she shakes me off and takes a step back. "No. I don't accept it."

It's my turn to be confused. "You can't not accept it. It's the way it is. I... I don't want to be with you anymore."

Her face starts to go red and I know she's about to cry before the tears start flowing. "This isn't happening. This isn't happening," she murmurs.

I am a shit sandwich. I want to pull her into my arms and comfort her, but I'm positive she won't let me. Why would she? I'm the person inflicting the pain. "I'm so sorry. I should've done this a while ago. It hasn't been fair to you to be with me when I'm not the right guy for you. I just didn't want to hurt you." I feel a pang as I realize Krissa said the exact same thing to me yesterday on Main Street. Krissa didn't want to hurt me, or Owen, or anyone else. I don't want to hurt Dana. Unfortunately, there's no way not to.

Dana stares me right in the eye. "If you don't want to hurt me, why are you breaking up with me?"

Before I can answer, she dissolves into tears. She bends at the waist, leaning so far forward I'm afraid she might fall, but when I reach for her, she pulls away.

"Don't touch me. Don't you ever touch me!"

I don't know what to do. I don't know what to say to make any of this better. As I spin through different options in my mind, I realize there's probably nothing I can say. "Do you want me to drive you home?"

She stands up and I don't have time to react before her fist comes down on my chest. She lands a few blows before backing away on her high heels and bumping into the coffee table as she stalks toward the door.

"You're an asshole, Fox Holloway! I never want to see you again!" She swings the door open so hard it slams against the adjacent wall. She doesn't bother closing it before stomping off the porch.

I follow. While I'm beyond positive she won't let me take her home, she's in no condition to make it there on her own. Maybe I could offer to call a cab? I've never done that—I don't even know if there is a cab company in Clearwater—but I at least want to offer.

She's nearly to my car by the time I make it onto the porch, and before I can call out, she brings her hands up in front of her like she plans to shove my truck. But she doesn't move near enough to touch it—instead, she stands about a foot away from it, her arms stretched out like a B-movie zombie. When I'm about to ask what she's doing, I'm cut off by an awful ripping, smashing sound as a wave of energy strikes the front corner of my truck and dents it, smashing the headlight.

I'm too shocked to react, and before I even manage to close my open mouth, Dana takes off at a run down the sidewalk, her high heels clip-clopping.

Chapter Twenty-Five
Krissa

Griffin presses a steaming mug of tea into my hands. By its aroma, I identify it as the anti-anxiety blend we sell at the shop. I offer him a small smile as he settles down next to me on his dilapidated couch.

Almost everyone I invited here today has arrived, and all eyes are on me. Tucker sits on Griffin's other side and has angled himself to see past him. Lexie and Bria sit on the dinged-up coffee table across from me, and Felix has dragged over a chair from the second-hand dining room set Griffin acquired since the last time I was here.

They're all waiting for me to say something, to explain why I've asked them all to come, but I'm not ready yet. I'm too nervous, and the Influence is taking full advantage of my heightened emotions.

Its hold on me hasn't ebbed since they stopped my heart the other night. The crackle of its energy is ever-present, a hum inside my body I can't turn off. I'm still wearing the ring we enchanted weeks ago, but I have a feeling it's not affecting the Influence anymore.

I take a sip of the tea, hissing when it burns my lips and my throat. It hurts, but at least it's a pain I can control.

Felix leans forward, resting his elbows on his thighs. "Okay, enough with the suspense. Why are we here?"

"And what's with the secrecy?" Bria adds. "You said you wanted to meet about a spell, and you made me promise not to tell anyone about it. Since we're not meeting at your house, I'm assuming Jodi doesn't know what you're up to."

"And where's Owen?" Lexie asks. "Is he running late, or..."

I shake my head. "I didn't want him here. He wouldn't let me go through with this."

There's a communal shifting in the room. "What are you asking us to do?" Tucker asks. "I mean, I think we've already proven we're willing to do whatever it takes to help you—but what can be worse than stopping your heart? Owen was fine with that, wasn't he?"

I take another sip of the tea before setting the mug on the floor. "The spell I want to try is complex, and there are some pretty serious consequences if it doesn't go right."

Griffin's eyebrows hike. "More serious than brain damage and death? I'll admit I'm intrigued." He attempts one of his casual, roguish smiles, but it looks more like a grimace.

He's nervous. A quick survey of their faces tells me they all are. I can't blame them. If I'd had my way, I wouldn't have consulted them at all, but this isn't a one-person spell.

Bria twists a ring on her finger. "If this spell is so hard, why didn't you ask more people to come? More witches? I mean, yeah, Griffin and Lexie can borrow energy from me and Felix and Tucker, but wouldn't it be easier to have more witches here? Or at least a stronger witch?"

Lexie nods. "Yeah, like Crystal."

The Influence flares, its flames licking at my insides. I've tried to fight it for weeks, but all my energy is now being directed at keeping the Influence in check, and I can't deny my anger toward Crystal anymore. Since the Influence spell, I've tried convincing myself she never meant for any of this to happen, that she was simply trying to keep her family safe from Brody and his threats. She was trying to learn the information he wanted so he would leave her alone. But I can't ignore the fact that she wanted her magic back so desperately she was willing to cast the spell despite my reservations.

"I can't have her here," I murmur.

Bria's face scrunches. "But wouldn't it help if—"

Red begins to encroach on my vision and I squeeze my eyes closed in an attempt to drive it back. "I know how strong her magic is," I say through clenched teeth. "It's *my* magic. I don't know if you realize how much it kills me to know that. She gets to walk around like nothing happened. She's got access to more power than she had to begin with. She can go on with her life, completely unaffected, while I have to endure spell after spell to try to rid myself of this... this *evil*."

A hand rests on my knee and gives a gentle squeeze. I'm able to take in a deep breath for the first time in what feels like minutes. When I open my eyes, the red is gone. I cover Griffin's hand with mine and offer a small smile. Although he's pale, he returns it. When I survey the room, I detect similar anxious looks on all my friends' faces and a wave of guilt swells in me. They don't deserve my anger. They've done nothing but try to help me. I don't want to scare them.

Before I can think of something to say to apologize for my outburst, my phone vibrates. I pull it out and smile when I see who it's from. "Besides," I say, standing and starting for the front door, "I did invite another witch."

I swing open the door to reveal Sasha, who stands, studying her nail beds as if I've taken forever to answer.

There's a scuffling of feet as she crosses the threshold. When I turn, everyone is standing.

"What the hell are you doing here?" Griffin growls. His face is a mask of fury, and I know I'm the reason.

"Down, boy," she responds easily, striding confidently forward as if nothing is amiss. "Don't worry—I come in peace."

Lexie turns to me with wide eyes. "Why did you invite her? It's her fault you're like this in the first place."

I understand my friends' confusion. It's hard to explain why I don't hold it against her. Yes, Sasha was the one who presented the Influence spell to Crystal. She's since admitted she did it in the hope Crystal would cast it and leave me to deal with the aftermath. She wanted to make my friend suffer so I would suffer. But something changed in her that night when Elliot found out what she was planning. She realized she'd gone too far. "She's trying to make up for that now," I say simply.

Felix crosses his arms over his chest. "How do we know whatever she's suggesting won't be as bad or worse than the Influence? We can't trust her."

At his accusation, Sasha flusters. Her nonchalant posture disappears, replaced by a straight-backed stance that makes even her small frame seem tall. "Because this time I don't have any secret agenda. Yes, when I told Crystal about the Influence spell I didn't tell her what it really was. But Krissa is fully aware of all the worst-case scenarios that go along with this spell." She takes another step forward, imitating Felix's pose. "Besides, in case you forgot, I'm the one who found the spell that's kept Krissa in control for this long." She reaches for my hand and holds it up so everyone can see my ring.

Tucker's expression clouds and he opens his mouth to shoot off another accusation, but I talk over him. "Look, everyone. I need your trust, and if you can trust me, you can trust Sasha." I sigh. I don't want to admit what I'm about to say, but my friends deserve to know. "I'm not okay. I know I keep saying I am, but I'm lying. I don't want anyone to worry about me.... You know, more than you already are. But since you guys stopped my heart the other night, it's like I can't ignore it anymore. It's always there, always one breath away from lashing out and hurting someone. I'm using every bit of energy and self-control to keep it in check, but I don't know how much longer I can do that." I reach for Sasha's hand and squeeze it. Her eyes widen in surprise, but she doesn't pull away. "I vouch for Sasha. I trust her. And she and I are going through with this spell whether you all help or not."

Griffin is the first to speak. "I'll help."

"Me, too," Felix says quickly.

One by one, the others agree. I turn to Sasha and smile. She offers a curt nod in return, and once she's released my hands, she surreptitiously wipes beneath her eyes before crossing to the table to snag a chair for herself.

We all settle into our seats and I turn to Sasha, encouraging her with my eyes to explain the spell.

"I understand you've tried some things lately to get the Influence out of Krissa. You tried exorcising it. You tried killing her so it would leave." She shakes her head at the last one, and for the first time, I wonder how she would have reacted if I hadn't come back from that spell. "Now, I'm not saying there isn't a way to get the Influence out for good, but I haven't been able to find anything yet. So, in the short term, I suggest we separate the Influence from Krissa's consciousness. It'll still be inside her, but it'll be buried down deep."

"Like a split personality?" Bria asks. When Felix raises an eyebrow, she holds up her hands innocently. "We were talking about dissociative identity disorder in psychology a couple weeks ago."

Felix snorts, but Sasha is nodding. "Yeah. The spell can bury a bad personality flaw or a trauma until the person is ready to deal with it. It kind of builds a wall between the dominant personality and whatever they want to separate from themselves."

Lexie's face scrunches in the same way it does when she's trying to work out a particularly complex math equation. "This sounds pretty good, actually. But it can't be that easy. What are the dangers?"

Sasha presses her lips together and glances at me.

"I might not be strong enough," I say. "There's a very real possibility the Influence won't be the consciousness that gets locked away. In which case I turn into a remorseless killing machine." I force a smile, but no one returns it.

"We won't let that happen," Tucker says matter-of-factly. He nods toward Felix and Bria. "We can guide you while the witches do the spell. We can make sure you're the one who stays on the surface." But when he glances at me, he can't quite mask the fear in his eyes. "I mean, that's possible, right?"

I've done similar things before—guiding people's consciousness to the surface after spells left them knocked out. "Yeah, it's possible," I agree, even though I'm not confident things will work the same in this situation.

But my assurance is all anyone seems to need. Griffin asks Sasha to go over the spell, and she explains it. My mind begins to whir. I'm more scared about doing this spell than I was the other night when they stopped my heart. If they hadn't been able to get my blood pumping again, at least I would've taken the Influence with me. But if this spell doesn't go as planned, the darkness within me won't be restricted anymore, and there's no telling what might happen then.

Instead of making me lie on the floor, Sasha directs me to recline on the couch. My heart hammers in my chest and blood rushes in my ears. I don't want to go through with this, but I have to.

Bria kneels beside me and takes my hand. "I'll be right here," she murmurs.

I'm thankful for her presence, though part of me wants to tell her to back away in case the spell goes wrong. But I can't go into this thinking negatively, so I squeeze her hand. She returns the pressure. I have to believe this will work, that I'll be the one who comes out in control.

When the spell begins, I feel nothing out of the ordinary. Even the Influence remains at a steady level as it sizzles beneath the surface of my skin. I'm not sure how aware the energy is, but at the very least, it doesn't appear to sense any danger. I concentrate on my breathing exercises. Breathe in. Hold. Breathe out.

Slowly, my brain begins to cloud over. I lose count, but my breathing stays even. I'm no longer afraid. No thoughts spin through my mind. I simply am.

By degrees, I realize I'm not alone. There's another presence nearby, but I can't see it. There is only white. It would be nice to stay here. There's no crackling or burning sensations, no guilt, no fear.

My weightless presence takes on mass and I begin sinking slowly, but I don't mind. The sensation is pleasant. As I drop lower, I begin to feel sleepy. I should rest. I should nap. In fact, I deserve a long, long sleep. I can go someplace where no one will be able to interrupt me.

Then my downward progress stops abruptly, shaking a measure of the sleepy sensation away. There are tugs at my consciousness. Ideas that are not my own attempt to penetrate my mind. *Don't sleep. You have to stay awake. You have to stay with us.*

Despite the urgency of the thoughts, I don't want to do what they say. I'm tired, so very tired. I've been working so hard to be normal these last few weeks—all I want to do is go somewhere to rest. Why can't they understand that? I'll rest, and when I wake up, everything will be normal.

When I wake up... But... I won't wake up. This isn't normal sleep. If I disappear now, who knows when I'll return. *If* I'll return.

The tugs on my consciousness grow stronger and I stop fighting them. They're right. I can't sleep—not here, not now. I need to fight now, just one more time.

The cloudiness evaporates from my mind like fog disappearing in the light of day. I'm aware of my body, of the rough fabric of Griffin's couch.

Griffin. I'm in his apartment with some of my closest friends. They're here to help me.

I open my eyes, only to close them again immediately against the harsh lamplight coming from near my feet. Was the lamp on earlier? I thought it was brighter when we began the spell, but a glance out the window reveals the fading light of late evening.

I sit up and my head spins. I press my hands into the couch cushions to keep from tipping over. "What's happening? How long was I out?"

Lexie and Bria, who sit on the floor in front of the couch, let out identical sighs of relief. Felix sits down beside me and pulls me into a tight hug. "Don't you ever scare me like that again, you hear?"

I return his embrace as best I can, but I don't understand what's happening. I glance around the room until I lock eyes with Tucker, whose typically disheveled hair is mussed to a whole new level, like he's been running his hands through it nervously for hours. My stomach clenches when I realize it's entirely possibly he has been. "We almost lost you," he says, his voice tight.

"It is *you*, right?" Griffin asks. His eyes slide to Tucker, who nods.

"Was there some doubt?" I attempt to smile, but there's no merriment in anyone's eyes, only cautious relief.

Sasha sits on my other side. I only realize Felix is still hugging me when she gently removes his arms from around me. "It's been hours since we started the spell. I had to text your dad because he sent a couple texts, asking when you'd be home." Alarm bells go off in my head, but before I can voice my concern, she's talking again. "I pretended to be you. Said you were at Bria's house studying for finals with some friends."

Bria hefts herself off the floor and settles on the coffee table. "The spell went pretty smoothly, from what the witches say," she explains. "But when it was over, there was no one in your head." She shrugs. "I'm not really sure how to explain it. It's like your body couldn't figure out who should be in control."

Felix takes my hand and squeezes it. "Your consciousness wasn't *gone*, but it wasn't... active."

"And then we started to lose you," Tucker says, settling down on a dining room chair. "You got fainter and fainter, like you were giving up."

I swallow. I'm trying to remember any of this happening, but my recollections are nebulous. "Thanks for not letting me."

"Now, for the real question," Sasha says, scrutinizing my face. "Did it work?"

At first, I think she's joking. Obviously it worked because I'm the one talking right now, not the Influence. But then it strikes me what she's really asking. For the first time since coming to, I take stock of my body, of the sensations coursing through it.

There is no thrum of electricity, no crackle of energy, no rising heat.

"I don't feel it." A laugh bubbles up from my stomach. "I don't feel the Influence at all."

After a beat, the room erupts into cheers. Felix hugs me again. Griffin offers beer to any interested parties. Lexie and Bria begin chattering at the same time about how excited they are.

All I can do is smile as I take it all in. Like Sasha said, this isn't a permanent solution, but it might just buy me enough time until we can figure one out.

Chapter Twenty-Six
Brody

I'm sitting in my car on a street perpendicular to Main. It's been days since my last conversation with Jade, and my stomach has been in knots since then. I have a plan, but I won't be satisfied until it's set in motion—until I can watch things begin to fall into place.

I will not lose out on my destiny because of Krissa Barnette. I have worked hard for decades to finally be in the position to take over as leader of the Amaranthine, and I refuse to let anything get in the way. If Krissa's reluctance to join me is tied to her misguided dream of having a happily-ever-after, that won't be an obstacle for long.

The passenger door opens and a boy with thick blond hair and deep-set eyes slides into the seat. West Harmon. His eyes are glazed, and a smile curves my lips. Good. Exactly as I anticipated. When I drew the summoning circle the vehicle now sits upon, I added in a few runes to cause confusion and compliance.

It was more difficult than I expected coming up with the three items to draw him here. It would have been much easier if it were Owen Marsh or Fox Holloway I needed to summon, but of course, that simply wouldn't do.

I hand a folded piece of paper to West. "Read it."

He opens it and stares, slightly slack-jawed, until he's absorbed the words. When he's finished, he shoves the paper back at me.

"Do you understand what you're supposed to do?"

He nods mutely. Without waiting for further instructions, he opens the car door and steps out into the Sunday afternoon sunshine, joining the dozens of people milling about—walking dogs, window shopping, enjoying the weather. I watch him until he disappears around the corner.

I could simply sit here, confident in the fact that West will do as instructed, but the temptation to watch the first domino fall is too strong. I cast a glamor before stepping out of the car, and a heavy, balding forty-year-old man follows West into the Wide Awake Cafe, not me. Besides my target, I doubt anyone else in here would recognize me, but it's always better to be safe. By the time I slide into a chair at a table near the one Owen occupies, West is already sitting across from him. I modify my glamor to make it look as if I'm holding a mystery novel and tune my attention to the conversation about to take place.

Owen's brow is pulled together with concern. "Dude, you okay? You seem a little... upset."

West rubs the back of his neck and shifts in his seat. I had no doubt my spell would hold, but I can't help smiling. It's always good to witness something play out exactly as I envisioned it. "I have to tell you something, and you're not going to like it. I've been wrestling with this for days. I don't want to say anything because it's not really my place, but you're my friend." He pauses for dramatic effect. "It's about Krissa."

"Is she okay?" Owen moves like he's about to stand and run. A knight in shining armor. I can guarantee he won't feel that way for long.

All evidence to the contrary, I'm actually a fan of true love. It's a pity I have to be instrumental in its demise, but it's for the greater good. The future of the Amaranthine is more important than the lives of a handful of teenagers.

"She's fine," West says.

Owen settles back down, his posture more relaxed. "I think I know what this is about. She's been different for the last few days, and I have a feeling it's because she did some kind of spell—something to do with the Influence. Something not sanctioned by Jodi. She hasn't mentioned anything about it to me, but I can tell she's doing better than she was. Were you there? Do you know what she did? Whatever it is, I'm not mad. It seems to be helping. She seems to be back to her old self."

West shakes his head. "I wish it were something that simple." There's a halting hesitation in his tone that makes Owen sit at attention. "I'm sorry—this is kind of hard to say. I've been trying to figure out the best way to tell you, but no matter what, it's going to suck. I guess I'm just gonna have to do it—like ripping off a bandage."

Owen's eyes narrow in confusion. "You're not making any sense."

"She's cheating on you, man," West says over Owen's words.

Owen stills as he processes the words. He tilts his head. After a beat, he cracks a smile. "You know, you actually had me going for a second." His expression turns dark, serious. "It's not funny, West."

"No, it's not," West agrees. "I wish I were joking. I was coming out of the bookstore a few days ago and I saw her talking with Fox. At first, I didn't think anything of it. I mean, they're friends, right? But then I overheard what they were saying. Fox was going on about how he didn't want to keep their relationship a secret anymore and how it was time for her to break up with you. Then she was saying how she had her reasons for keeping things from you." He presses his lips together. "I hate to be the one to tell you, but you deserve to know."

Owen shoves the palms of his hands against the edge of the table and shakes his head, as if doing so could dislodge the words he's hearing. "No. No, you're lying. I don't know why, but you are. There's no way. There's no way she'd do that to me."

"I wish it was a lie, man, but it's not. I just... I figured you should know."

Owen bangs a fist on the tabletop before standing and stalking out of the coffee shop. West remains immobile for several seconds before blinking heavily and shaking his head. He looks around with obvious uncertainty. He has no memory of arriving here. I murmur an incantation for a confusion charm—one just strong enough to get him back to doing whatever he was engaged in before the summoning spell brought him to me. He stands and slowly wanders toward the door.

A smile stretches across my lips. So much for Krissa's happy ending.

Chapter Twenty-Seven
Fox

My eyes are on Krissa's driveway. Any minute, her parents should be leaving to for their weekly Sunday afternoon date. Jodi is at the shop. One of the reasons Krissa and I have spent the last several Sundays together is because there wasn't anyone around to wonder where she was for hours on end.

But she's not coming to me today—I'm coming to her.

The cloaking spell I cast around my truck appears to be holding. No less than three dog walkers have passed by and not one has glanced in my direction. Even the dogs have passed by without so much as a sniff.

I drum my fingers on the steering wheel to get out some of my nervous energy. It's been days since I've spoken to Krissa. Her attendance at school has been hit or miss lately—not that school is the best place to have the kind of conversation I'm aiming for. Our talk on the street the other day didn't go so well, so another meeting like that is out, too. That leaves me only one choice—this choice. I need to talk to her somewhere private, where we won't be overheard. We need to get this whole thing straightened out.

Ben and Amy Barnette exit the house. I'm too far away to tell for sure, but I'm positive they're smiling. According to Krissa, they've been acting like newlyweds. I guess I can't blame them—they're making up for lost time, after all. And their penchant for romance is suiting my needs, so I support it fully.

Once their car pulls out of the driveway and down the street, I open my truck's door and start for the house, dropping the cloaking spell as I go.

I could knock, but I don't want to give her the opportunity to slam the door in my face. I try the handle and smile: it's unlocked, as always.

The first floor is quiet. She's not in the living room or dining room, and she usually only uses the sitting room when the house is full and she wants to be alone. That leaves only one place she could be.

I ascend the stairs, avoiding the creaky ones out of habit. I can't count the number of times I've been up this flight over the years.

When I reach the third floor, Krissa is bent over her desk. She's writing in a notebook that's too small to be for school. I consider crossing the room and tapping her shoulder, but I'm not sure how she'll react to that, so I settle for clearing my throat.

She jumps and spins, closing the notebook as she turns away from it. When her eyes land on me, her expression goes from surprised to upset. "You shouldn't be here. I thought I made myself clear last time we talked."

I take a few steps into her room. "You said you were sick of lying. I am, too. I wanted you to know I ended things with Dana."

She stands and brings a hand to her forehead. "You didn't need to do that."

"Yes, I did." I edge nearer to her. I want to close the distance entirely, but now isn't the moment. "I don't love her, Krissa. I love you. I've tried fighting it, but I can't. And you can't either." I take another step forward and reach for her, but she pulls away.

"I'm not fighting anything," she says, but I detect a tremble in her voice. "I'm with Owen. I chose him. In case you forgot, I ended things with you."

Her words sting, but I don't give up. "You said that because you're feeling guilty. I can't blame you. But you don't have to be afraid of telling the truth." I try to catch her eye, but she stares at the floor. "I'm sure you have feelings for him left over from your old reality, but you were never meant to be with him here. You're supposed to be with me."

She shakes her head. "I don't know how to be any clearer. Me being with you—it was a mistake. It was never what I wanted."

I take another step forward and brush my finger under her chin so she'll look up at me. "I know you love me. You can't deny it. I know it's true."

She steps back, pain flashing in her eyes. "But I *don't*."

I flinch, but I'm still not ready to give up. She can't deny what's been happening between us these last few weeks. I don't know why she suddenly has cold feet about us, but her feelings for me can't have evaporated. She's conflicted—it's plain as day on her face. "Then say it. I need to hear the words. If you can say to my face that you don't care about me at all, I'll believe you."

She opens her mouth, but no sound comes out. Hesitation flickers across her face. This has to be so hard for her. I know she's a good person, and she must feel loyalty to Owen because he remembers the other reality she experienced, but it's obvious she still has strong feelings for me. That's why she can't say she doesn't love me. It's not what's in her heart.

Any lingering doubts disappear from my mind. She can't deny it any more than I can: We're supposed to be together. I lean down and press my lips to hers.

"So it's true," says a voice.

Krissa pulls back and we both turn toward the stairs, where Owen is standing, glaring at us.

Chapter Twenty-Eight
Krissa

My mind is spinning. The heat from Fox's kiss is fresh on my lips and I fight the urge to wipe it away. But even if I did, it wouldn't erase what Owen just saw.

"It's not what you think," I say quickly. "Let me explain."

The anger from a moment ago fades from Owen's face, replaced by the blank expression of a man struggling to accept reality. "There's nothing you can say. I didn't want to believe it, but..."

Fox is still standing too close to me. He rubs the back of his neck. "Sorry, man. I know this won't mean much, but I never wanted you to find out like this."

In a flash, Owen lunges for him, but I'm so close to Fox I'm able to come between them. Behind me, Fox jostles as though he'd like nothing better than to get around me and give Owen the fight he wants. I brace myself for the red smoke of the Influence to begin twisting in on my vision, but it doesn't come. I don't even feel a prickle of energy. The dissevering spell is holding—thank goodness. If it weren't, I don't want to imagine what kind of damage it could do in a situation like this.

"Fox, leave."

He shakes his head. "No. I don't like the idea of you being alone with him right now."

Irritation flares and I round on him. "Get out of here!"

He hesitates, obviously weighing his desire to stay against my insistence that he leave. After a beat, he nods and heads for the stairs.

When I hear the front door open and close, I turn to Owen. He's just as angry as he was when he was going after Fox. "Sit down. Please. Give me a chance to explain."

He won't look at me. "I don't know why I'm surprised," he murmurs.

I step forward, not sure I heard him right. Is it possible he sensed something like this was going on? Maybe he did, but he was in denial. I should've come clean as soon as I found out what was happening. It would have been better than him walking in on what he just saw. "Owen..."

He backs toward my desk like he intends to sit on the chair, but he remains standing. "When I first started getting the memories of us together, I wanted us to pick up where we left off in the other reality—and you hesitated. I finally get why. You didn't want to pick him or pick me—you wanted both of us. You refused to choose just one of us because you're seriously that selfish."

His words cut through me like a knife. "You can't really believe that," I insist, my face flushing. "I want you—I choose you. Whatever was going on with Fox—it wasn't me. It was the Influence. I had no idea it was even happening until about a week ago. As soon as I realized, I ended things with him."

Owen snorts. "The Influence. What a convenient excuse. Tell me, who else has the Influence been making you screw around with? Griffin? Tucker? Felix? Has it been making you hook up with them, too?"

Tears sting my eyes, but I make no effort to blink them away. I hate that he thinks I'm capable of something like that, but given the circumstances, I can't entirely blame him. Being with Fox may not have been my fault, but keeping it quiet was.

He closes the distance between us and stares into my eyes. "Tell me you don't love him. Tell me you don't have any feelings for him."

I want to tell him what he wants to hear. I want to confirm that he's the only one I love, that there's no room in my heart for anyone else, but it's not that easy. "I don't love him—not like I love you."

Owen's jaw clenches and his eyes harden. He grabs my wrist and begins untying the bracelet that keeps my mind sealed off from psychic intrusion. I don't fight him. I want him to see how conflicted my mind is. How true for him my love is.

Once the bracelet is removed, I wait for the sensation of another consciousness pressing against mine, but I don't feel anything. Of course I don't—that part of me is gone.

I watch his face as he scans my mind, but what I see on it isn't encouraging. I don't know exactly what he's picking up, but whatever it is, it's not good.

He turns his head and presses the bracelet back into my hand. "Goodbye, Krissa."

He starts for the stairs and I follow him. "Owen, wait. Don't go. I'll make it up to you—I promise I will."

He pauses at the top of the stairs and turns to face me. "That's the thing. I don't think you can."

Before I can respond, he's descending the stairs, moving farther and farther from me with each step.

Chapter Twenty-Nine
Brody

I'm back in my hotel room when my phone rings. For the first time since my arrival in Clearwater, I'm happy Jade is calling.

After leaving the cafe, I drove past Krissa's house. When I saw Fox's truck down the street and Owen's car in the driveway, I knew my plan was coming together. I'm more confident than I've been in some time.

I accept the call and Jade's face fills my phone screen. My usual smile comes easily. "Jade. So glad you called."

She doesn't look nearly as pleased to see me. "Your time is almost up, Brody, and no amount of charm is going to change that. Have you made any progress? Will the Amaranthine have their assassin?"

"Yes," I say emphatically. "About an hour ago, I set a plan in motion. All that's left for me to do is to wait for its effects to take hold. I anticipate Krissa seeking me out within the next twenty-four hours."

Jade inhales through her nose. "I'm tired of waiting. It seems all you do in Clearwater is assure me something is about to happen. Last time you were there, you assured me you would get Bess Taylor's information. And before you try to remind me that you did, remember it came at a high price. The only reason you're there now is because your actions led to the death of our assassin. I need to be able to trust that your plan will work without any further complications."

My swell of positivity ebbs at her tone. "Tell me what you need to know. I'm happy to provide the—"

She shakes her head. "I've sent someone to oversee the rest of your operation. We have no room for missteps."

I'm about to ask who she sent when a knock sounds at my door. She nods, indicating I should answer it. When I pull it open, it takes every bit of my composure to keep my anger off my face. Lena Wiley stands in the hall. Her smirk lets me know she can sense my displeasure.

"Lena is reporting directly to me."

Jade's voice startles me. I forgot she was still on the phone. "I am reporting directly to you," I say, keeping my voice as even as possible.

She ignores my comment. "Now that we're all together, I'd like to hear your plan."

Lena invites herself in and closes the door behind her. I lead the way to the suite's small sitting area, and she takes the armchair I'm partial to. I narrow my eyes as I sit on the couch. "I've learned what's holding Krissa back. She's obsessed with the idea of living in ordinary life. She wants to be happy and in love like the teenagers on TV. However, it seems she wants love a little too much. She's been stringing two boys along, and I informed the boyfriend in the dark that she's been cheating on him. He's at her house as we speak, no doubt breaking up with her because he caught her in flagrante with the other boy. Once she realizes her dream life is simply that, there won't be anything holding her back from joining us." I sit up straighter, waiting for Jade to praise me for my brilliance, but it doesn't come.

"That's your plan?" she asks, her tone measured. "And you are confident it's going to work?"

Lena snorts. "Of course it won't work. Yes, it's possible the boyfriend has broken up with her, but so what? What's to keep them from working it out and getting back together next week? She's been seeing two boys, has she not? If one rejects her, there's still the other to run to." She leans forward and snatches the phone from my hand. "We don't have an assassin yet because he's not willing to do what's necessary," she says to the screen. "If this were my assignment, Krissa would be on our side already."

"I doubt that," I say through clenched teeth.

"Try me." There's a hard look in her eyes that I recognize. I've seen it in my own many times. She's set her sights on impressing Jade, and she's not going to let anything stop her. I knew the girl was bold, but I didn't think she was capable of these kinds of maneuvers.

"I'll leave you two to work things out," Jade says. "But remember, Brody, we're counting on you. Our future—and yours—depends on the outcome of this mission."

Three beeps signal the end of the call. Lena slaps my phone down on the low coffee table and smirks, clearly happy with the implication of Jade's words. "I've been in the car for too long. I'm going to my room to shower, and when I come back, I want to hear all the details of your *genius* plan. I mean, it has to be more complex than what you told Jade, doesn't it?" She rolls her eyes as she stands and struts toward the door.

My blood is boiling by the time she's out of the room. My suspicions were right—she has been getting into Jade's good graces in my absence. Is it really possible that Jade is considering putting her support behind Lena as her successor? She's a child. She doesn't have the experience necessary to lead the Amaranthine.

But if she's the one who's able to convince Krissa to become our assassin, it's possible she could play down her inexperience and point to how she was able to succeed when someone more seasoned failed.

I can't fail. As much as I hate to admit it, Lena brought up a good point: What's to stop Krissa from simply cutting her losses and deciding to be with Fox instead of Owen? Or what's to keep Owen from deciding he'll forgive her? As much as I thought my plan was bulletproof, I suppose there are some holes in it.

I'll simply have to shore them up. It's not enough to cause a rift between her and the one she loves; I have to take it further. I have to make sure there's nothing for her to go back to.

I stand and begin pacing the room. The question now becomes how far is too far? Is there such a thing?

Of course there isn't. I'm willing to go as far as it will take to force Krissa's hand and make her accept my offer. In fact, I'm going to go farther—as far as possible. I don't want to leave any chance for her to have the life she thinks she wants.

I'm going to take away any hope she has of her happy ending. I'll crush any chance for the normal life she dreams of.

Chapter Thirty
Krissa

It's the first day of finals, and Owen didn't show up in second hour. It's completely out of character for him to skip something so important, no matter how mad he might be.

I'm worried. I can't believe he's so upset he can't even bring himself to be in the same class with me for ninety minutes. Was he afraid I'd try to talk to him? Would I have tried? I don't think I would have attempted it in the middle of our science exam, but I can't say for sure. It's killing me that I haven't gotten the chance to explain things to him. I tried texting him after he left my house, but there was no response. Not that I was expecting one. He's angry, and rightfully so. I know he needs time to process things, but I can't help wanting to plead my case one more time. If he'd give me even five minutes, I'm sure I could make him see I never intended to hurt him.

I hope.

I know I should give him space, but unease sits like a rock in the pit of my stomach. While I suppose it's possible he made arrangements with Mrs. Bates to take the final in another room or at another time, I can't shake the feeling that something is wrong.

As soon as the bell rings, instead of going to clean out my locker as I was directed, I scurry to my car and point it in the direction of Owen's house. Maybe it's a bad idea to go there to check on him, but I can't convince myself not to. If showing up unannounced makes him angrier with me, I'll deal with it when the time comes. I just need to know he's okay.

Neither his parents' cars nor Owen's Grand Prix is in the driveway, but that doesn't mean no one is home. Maybe Owen had car trouble. Maybe his car is in the garage. My mind grasps at any possible explanation as I pull to a stop in front of his house.

I peer in through the front window as I climb the porch stairs. I don't detect any movement inside, but I knock on the door anyway. When there's no response, I knock again, even though I don't expect anyone to answer. After checking over my shoulders to be sure no one is watching, I try the handle, murmuring a little prayer of thanks when I find it unlocked.

As I slip inside, a voice in the back of my mind points out I'm probably overstepping here. What if Owen's parents come home while I'm sneaking around like a burglar? I've met them, of course, but what if Owen told them we're fighting? I don't know if I'll be able to come up with a good excuse for prowling around their house.

Heart thudding in my chest, I move through the rooms as quickly and quietly as possible. As I suspected, no one is home. But if Owen's not here, where could he be? Never before have I wished so fervently I could cast a locater spell. Of course, there's no way for me to do that. Even if I were desperate enough to tap into the Influence, I can't do that anymore. The Influence is locked away in a deep recess of my mind now. Since the dissevering spell, the constant simmering just beneath the surface of my skin has disappeared entirely. I've felt more like myself than I have in months—since before the night Seth died.

Since magic is out, I'll have to find him the old-fashioned way.

I peek out the front window before exiting the house. The street is just as still as it was when I entered. I jog to my car and head for downtown. Owen spends a lot of time at the coffee shop. Maybe he's there now. For the moment, it's the best guess I have.

I park on Main across from the cafe and climb out of the car, but before I can cross the street, I catch sight of Dana. It's not too unusual to see her around here, so that's not what surprises me— it's the hurt in her eyes that roots me to my spot. When she sees me, she stalks straight for me.

I open my mouth to ask her what's wrong, but before I can get a word out, she winds up and slaps me across the face. I'm too shocked to move. My mind spins, landing on the fact that Dana is damn lucky the dissevering spell worked, because if she'd hit me before it was locked away, I doubt I could have kept the Influence from incinerating her on the spot. Even now, despite the spell's effects, it rustles gently in the back of my consciousness, reminding me of its presence. It's barely strong enough to register—the first time I've sensed it since the spell.

Before I recover enough to ask what's happening, Dana starts yelling. "I had my suspicions when Fox broke up with me, but I figured I'd give you the benefit of the doubt. After all, I thought this version of you wasn't a backstabbing whore. Guess I was wrong."

I try to swallow, but my throat is dry. Even after I realized what was going on with Fox and me—after I told him not to break up with her—I never really considered the fallout if she found out what was happening. "What did Fox tell you?"

Does she have the whole story? Does she think I was actively attempting to steal him from her? Either way, I suppose her anger is valid, but I need her to understand I never went out of my way to hurt her. If she can understand, maybe Owen can, too.

Her lip curls at the sound of his name on my lips. "Him? Nothing. I haven't seen him. But Owen caught up with me between finals to inform me I should dump Fox since he's been cheating with you. I guess he didn't get the memo Fox already dumped me."

The stinging on my cheek dissipates and a bubble of hope rises in my chest. "You saw Owen today? He wasn't in second hour."

She glares at me. "Maybe he didn't want to see your cheating bitch-face."

"Or maybe he was detained."

Dana and I both jump at the male voice, but I know who it belongs to before I turn.

Brody.

Dana shrinks back, taking a half step behind me. She's using me as a human shield, and I can't blame her. "Why are you here? Crystal gave you the information you wanted—you were supposed to leave town."

Brody doesn't look the slightest bit uneasy. He could simply be out for a walk, taking in the sunshine on this warm spring day— except he's not. That's not the kind of person he is. If he's here, it can only mean trouble. "I did leave," he says, his voice casual. "Now I'm back."

I don't have the time or patience to wait for Dana to adjust to Brody's presence in town. "What do you mean, detained? What did you do with Owen?"

He shrugs and leans back against the hood of my car, crossing his arms over his chest. "He's safe—for now. And so is Fox."

Dana lunges forward, but not far enough to actually strike out at Brody. Despite her anger, she seems to sense she wouldn't come off the better in a fight against him. "Don't hurt him." Her tone is more command than request.

Brody holds up his hands, but the curl of his lips belies his feigned innocence. "I think the two of them have been sufficiently hurt by Krissa, wouldn't you agree? Despite what she claims—even to herself—it seems her heart is torn between the two of them. I've simply devised a way to encourage her to be honest with herself. Owen and Fox are hidden away somewhere in Clearwater, and both will die in exactly"—he checks his watch—"one hour and twenty-eight minutes, unless she chooses the one she loves the most."

My decision is automatic. I don't even have to think about it. It's Owen, of course. I care about Fox—there's no denying that—but

Owen is the one my heart longs for. I belong with him.

I open my mouth to tell Brody who I've chosen, but Dana cuts me off. "What happens to the other one?"

Brody grins, flashing teeth. "He gets taken out of the equation. Whoever Krissa picks won't have to worry about her affections straying to the other when that other is dead."

Dana lets out a little yelp, and a wave of nausea swells in my stomach. I can't choose Owen if it means Fox will die. I may not want to be with him in the way he hopes, but I can't be the reason he's murdered by this psychopath.

"How do I save them both? There has to be a way." I have a feeling I already know the answer. Brody hasn't orchestrated this whole thing in some twisted attempt at helping me be true to myself. He's here for a reason, and there's no way he's giving up on it.

Brody's dark eyes fix on me. "If you agree to join me, both boys will live."

It's the answer I expected. He can't make me go willingly, so he's come up with this elaborate plan to force me into it. But I can't do it—even if it means saving Owen and Fox. There has to be another way. "Never. I won't be your assassin."

"Have it your way," Brody says, shrugging as if my answer is of no consequence to him. "Try to find them. But I warn you, my magic is strong and the enchantments concealing them are hard to break. Be my guest, though; I'll be waiting at our usual meeting place when you realize my way is the only way to save them."

I stare at him for a beat longer. There's no doubt in my mind he'll make good on his threats. Although last time he was in town, Kai was the one who did all the dirty work, I know it was all on Brody's orders. He was willing to kill Crystal's parents to get information from her. He's heartless, and pleading or reasoning with him will have no effect.

I turn to my car and pull open the driver's side door. My fingers tremble, and I drop the key twice before managing to slide it into the ignition. I feel Brody's eyes on me until I start the car; only then does he walk away.

Before I can put the car in gear, the passenger door swings open and Dana slides into the seat. "You have a plan, right? You have to do something. You have to find Fox. Don't forget it's your fault he's in this mess anyway."

Does she think I don't know that? I'm fully aware that two people I care about are in danger simply because of their proximity to me. There's a prickle in the deep recesses of my mind, but I ignore it. I won't let the Influence rise up and take over, no matter how much it may want to.

"I know it's my fault," I say, my voice low as I pull onto the street. "I'll save them both, but we're going to need magic to find them. I can't use the Influence. We'll need help."

Chapter Thirty-One
Fox

My skin is warm and slick with sweat. I try to open my eyes, but my eyelids are heavy. Have I overslept? Did I miss my finals? My heartbeat picks up as panic sets in. But no—I woke up and went to school. I remember going to my first exam. It was easier than I thought it would be.

I try to bring my hand up to rub the sleep from my eyes, but my arm won't move. For a split second, I assume it's asleep, but then I feel the bite and scratch of rope against my wrists.

I finally manage to open my eyes, but when I do, I'm even more confused. I'm standing, and my arms are tied behind my back. Another rope encircles my chest—probably the only thing that kept me upright while I was unconscious. I'm outside and the sun is beating down from almost directly overhead. On the ground all around me are thick, green shoots.

Corn. I'm in a cornfield.

Who the hell would tie me up in a cornfield? The first idea that comes to mind is completely insane—that Dana did it to get back at me for breaking up with her. But of course, that's crazy.

There's movement about a hundred yards in front of me. Someone is walking through the field. She probably owns this place and is wondering what I'm doing out here. I open my mouth to call out, but my throat is dry. I wonder how long I was unconscious. I struggle to swallow before trying again. "Help! Help me!"

She sees me—it's impossible that she doesn't, because her eyes are fixed directly on me—yet my calls don't hasten her pace. She continues to move slowly, methodically, her eyes never wavering from my face.

As she nears, I start wondering if my initial assessment was incorrect. She doesn't look like a farmer. Her clothes are too sleek. While she wears jeans, they're clearly expensive, and her low-cut red tank top isn't the kind a person would wear while tending fields. Her hair is loose around her shoulders, not pulled back like it would be if she planned to work in the hot sun for any length of time.

But if she's not a farmer, what is she doing here? Why is she in this field with me? Maybe she noticed me as she was passing by— but her movements don't indicate any concern for my well-being.

It's not until she's about two yards away that I realize she's definitely not here to help me. Her green eyes are cold and calculating. She continues walking until she is less than an arm's length from me, her gaze fixed on me the whole way.

She reaches out and I flinch, but all she does is gently stroke my cheek. The gesture is in such contrast to the coldness in her eyes that I'm not sure how to react. "I hear you're the one she won't choose," she murmurs. "It must be a hard decision. You're both so... tempting." Her finger trails along my jaw before dropping to my chest and tracing a line down toward my stomach. "To be honest, I find you more attractive than the other boy, but I can't fault her for her choice. There's something about him—something special. Have you sensed it?"

All I can do is stare at her. I'm not sure whether she expects a response or not, but either way, I have none to give. My mind is spinning, trying to figure out what she's talking about and what's going on.

Her lips curve in a secretive smile. "Of course you haven't sensed it. You're not a psychic."

"But you are?" The question tumbles out of my mouth before I make the conscious decision to ask it. My voice is rough both from the yelling and the lack of moisture in my throat. Her finger is still tracing lines up and down my chest. I don't really want to engage her in conversation, but I do want to know exactly what the hell's happening to me. I'm positive now this has something to do with Krissa, but I have no idea what.

"Not exactly. I'm more sensitive than your average person, but I wouldn't call myself a full-blown psychic. And I've picked up some very interesting vibrations off that other boy. It's really too bad he won't be around long enough for me to figure out what makes him so unique."

More pieces snap together in my mind and my heart starts hammering again. If whatever is going on does have to do with Krissa, there's no doubt the other guy is Owen. What does she mean, he won't be around long? What about me? Whatever the reason I'm tied up, it can't be good. "What are you going to do to him?"

She taps her pointer finger on the tip of my nose. "Nothing you need to worry about."

It's not exactly an answer. "Why? Because you don't have the same thing in store for me?"

The smile drops from her face and she tilts her head to the side. "Because it'll be over before you have a chance to feel it."

Bile rises in my throat as the implication of her words sinks in. She spins on her heel and starts off the way she came before I can ask for clarification. By the time I find my voice, she's at least three yards away. "Why are you doing this? What's going to happen? Just let me go! Why can't you let me go?"

I yell the words until my throat burns, but she doesn't acknowledge me in any way. I watch as she walks to the road bordering the field and climbs into her car. I don't stop yelling until her car is out of sight.

My heart is thundering in my chest, and I can feel the blood surging through my veins. As much as I don't want to dwell on what her words meant, my mind can't help spinning through different scenarios, all of which end with me dead.

Another car drives down the road and I scream at the top of my lungs, hoping to call attention to myself. The road isn't too far off, probably less than a quarter mile—definitely close enough that the person driving with their window down should hear and see me. But the car continues as if there's nothing strange occurring in the field.

Magic. It's the only explanation. Of course this crazy lady wouldn't leave me in the middle of a field where anyone could find me. She probably cast cloaking charms to keep me from sight and incantations to keep my voice from carrying. Unless someone is specifically looking for me, I won't be found.

Owen is tied up like this somewhere, too. Although the woman didn't say his name, I have no doubt he's the other one. Does Krissa already know we've been taken? If so, which one of us is she looking for?

A heavy weight settles in the pit of my stomach when I realize it's not me. The thing I've been trying to ignore for weeks now, the real reason Krissa never wanted to come clean about the two of us being together, breaks into my consciousness, unwilling to be ignored any longer: Krissa doesn't want me.

These last few weeks, I've ignored any doubts or suspicions that have surfaced since she first came to me. I haven't been entertaining the idea that Krissa sincerely didn't want to be with me. But now I have no doubt that whatever brought her to me these last few weeks wasn't love. It was an anomaly. Krissa wants to be with Owen. Even that crazy woman knows it.

So why am I tied up in a field?

The answer comes to me in pieces. Even if it's true that Krissa will choose Owen, I know she cares for me. She's told me as much before—it's part of the reason I was able to believe she wanted to be with me. For some reason, she's being forced to choose between us in the most extreme way I can imagine. But when she chooses Owen, where will that leave me?

Chapter Thirty-Two
Krissa

"Dammit, dammit, dammit!" Griffin shouts, pounding his fist on the coffee table before standing and aiming a kick at the corner of his couch.

West lifts his head from the grimoire he's been studying. "Let me guess: the locater spell didn't work?"

Griffin points at him. "If you know what's good for you, psychic, you'll shut the hell up right now. I've been looking for an excuse to punch you since the binding spell."

Lexie stands from the dining room chair she's been perched on and positions herself between the two of them. "We don't really have time for this, do we?"

She's right, but I don't say anything. I can't say anything. Dana and I were both on the phone as soon as I started driving, contacting all the witches and psychics and asking them to meet at Griffin's place. Everyone got here as quickly as they could. Sasha brought a handful of grimoires, as did Crystal, who went an extra step and picked up the Barnette grimoire from my house on her way. The witches set to finding Owen and Fox with magic, while the psychics began scouring the books of spells.

But I'm not doing either. I'm standing here, in the corner of the room, in the same spot I got here. Guilt and fear keep me rooted. Guilt because everything that's happening is my fault and there's nothing I can do to help, and fear that my friends' efforts won't be enough. Fear that I'll lose two people I love because I'm unable to access magic to find them.

I'm useless.

I wish I had my magic back, even a small measure of it. A little bit of power right now would put me at ease.

Perhaps that's not entirely true. If I'm honest, I wish we hadn't done the dissevering spell. I wish I still had access to the Influence. Brody wants me to use it for him, but how would he react if I turned it against him? Unfortunately, no matter how much fear or anger I summon, I can't call forth the wisps of red smoke. The Influence is nothing more than a shadowy presence in the deepest recesses of my mind. It's not part of me anymore—it's a separate entity within me. If I let it take over, there's no promise I'll ever be able to come back.

"Obviously whoever took Fox put enchantments around him so a locater spell wouldn't work," Griffin says. Sasha already pointed out that would probably be the case, but it seems Griffin is finally coming to terms with the information. "We still need to find where Fox is being hidden."

"And Owen," Felix adds.

Griffin clenches his jaw but doesn't say anything. He doesn't have to. Fox is his brother—of course he's Griffin's priority.

"It's good we tried the locater spell," Sasha says, her voice measured. She's taking a different tack than she initially tried. Originally, she told Griffin he was naïve to think Brody would be stupid enough to let his plan be undone with a simple locater spell. I'm glad she's trying to be kinder now. Making Griffin angry isn't going to help us find either of them.

Crystal snorts, crossing her arms over her chest. "What's so good about it? It didn't work."

Sasha spares a brief withering look at Crystal before addressing the rest of the room. Bria, Tucker, and Dana look up from the grimoires they're studying. "It's probably safe to assume he's cast the usual enchantments—spells to keep anyone from seeing Fox or Griffin, or from hearing them when they yell for help. But the kind of cloaking spell required to hide a person's location from magic draws a lot of energy."

Bridget bites her lower lip. "So, he's really strong...?"

"We knew that already," Sasha says. "What I'm saying is, we might not be able to locate Fox and Owen, but we might be able to find out where they're being hidden."

"Would you stop talking in riddles?" Griffin snarls. "We can't find them but we can find where they are? Why are you here again?"

I've gotten to know Sasha well enough to catch the flash in her eyes. If we weren't on a deadline, I'm sure she'd give Griffin a piece of her mind. Instead, she takes in a deep breath and releases it slowly. "Brody is pulling a ton of magic to keep them hidden. Instead of looking for Fox and Owen, we can focus on finding the magic."

My skin prickles. Is she right? Could it be that easy? What she's saying makes sense. Except I have no idea how we'd go about it.

Tucker voices the same question an instant after it crosses my mind. "Is there a spell for that or something?"

Sasha's lips press together in a tight line. My heart sinks. If there is, she doesn't know of it off the top of her head.

West closes the book he's been reading and stands from his spot on the floor. "Maybe we don't need a spell."

Griffin's eyebrows hitch upward. "What do you mean?"

"Maybe we could try dowsing for it," West says, his voice unsure. "I've been reading about how psychics can use their abilities to dowse for things like water or oil. Why not magic?"

"You've been reading?" Bria asks.

West points at her. "Not the time for your sass. The point is, I think it might work. I just need a Y-shaped stick or rod."

No sooner have the words left West's mouth than Griffin darts from the living room. When he emerges from his bedroom seconds later, he holds up a wire hanger triumphantly. "Will this work?"

West nods. "It might."

Felix, who's closer to Griffin than West, relieves him of the hanger. Mere seconds after it's in his hand, it begins bending as he uses his telekinetic powers to form it into the correct shape.

Once it looks like a Y, Griffin takes it back and walks over to West. When he gives it to him, Griffin places a hand on West's shoulder. "Please find my little brother."

West nods grimly and turns toward the door, but before he can make it more than a few steps, Felix calls for him to wait before disappearing into Griffin's bedroom. He returns carrying more hangers and starts working them into the same shape as the one West is holding.

"We'll be more effective if we're all looking," Felix says, holding out a completed hanger toward Bria.

"That's a really good idea," Tucker says without any trace of sarcasm. He and Dana move to Felix's side for their own hangers. West joins them and starts explaining the process for dowsing.

Sasha calls the witches to her and explains that once a location is found, they will have to remove the enchantments that have been cast upon it. She casts a glamor on Griffin's coffee table and instructs each one how to do the spell to take it off.

I'm still standing in the corner, wishing there were anything I could do to help. But I can't. I can't wield magic and I can't sense energies. All I can do is sit here, steeping in my feelings, praying one of my friends will be able to undo my mess.

After Griffin successfully makes his coffee table reappear, he pulls his phone from his back pocket and checks the time. "That's going to have to be enough practice. We've gotta get moving."

Everyone begins pairing up—Crystal with Dana, Griffin with Tucker, Sasha with Bria, Bridget with West, and Lexie with Felix. Everyone has a partner except for me. I might as well be a statue.

Each set of partners exits the apartment. Only Lexie and Felix hang back, their eyes lingering on me.

"Why don't you come with us?" Felix asks.

I shake my head. "I won't be any help."

Felix and Lexie exchange glances. "It doesn't matter," Lexie says quickly. "It matters that we're looking. We'll find them."

I want to believe her, but the worry that's been gnawing at me bubbles to the surface. "And what if we don't? If we can't find them, Brody will make good on his threats." I can't bring myself to say the words "kill them," even though I know that will be their fate if we fail. I square my shoulders and step away from the corner for the first time since entering the apartment. "I can stop this. Brody gave me the way out. We don't have to hope these hangers can point us to magic—I can just—"

"Don't even think about it," Felix snaps. "It's not an option."

"But it is," I insist. "I'll do anything if it means saving the two of them."

Felix's jaw tightens and he postures like he's ready to argue, but Lexie places her hand on his arm. "We still have time," she says. "Have faith. There's nothing we've been up against so far that we haven't been able to overcome. Breaking the spell that anchored the witches to the crystal, defeating Seth, knocking back the Influence. We can do this, too."

I bite my lower lip, weighing her words. Yes, it's true we've been able to get ourselves out of many difficult situations, but this isn't the same. Still, I want to believe her. I slip my phone from my back pocket and check the time. "We should get going. We have fifty-three minutes."

Chapter Thirty-Three
Brody

I'm bored, and it's warmer than I'd like. I should have opted for a T-shirt rather than my usual button-down, but this will be over soon enough. I consider moving into my car for cover, perhaps turning on the air conditioning to combat the heat instead of staying here, leaning against the hood of my car. But before the thought is fully formed, my ears catch the sound of an engine in the distance. I smile. Krissa made her decision sooner than I anticipated. I figured she'd wait until the very last second before admitting there was no way she could save Owen and Fox without my help.

I turn, ready to greet her with open arms, but when I recognize the approaching car, my smile turns into a grimace. The flashy red coupe is Lena's. I stalk over to where she pulls to a stop. "What are you doing here?" I demand as soon as she opens the door.

She takes her time sliding out, studying me. What is she looking for? Signs of weakness or uncertainty? She'll find none. "Don't get your boxers in a twist," she finally says. "I've already seen to both boys. They're safe."

"That's not what I asked. You need to get back into position for phase two."

She slams the car door and leans against it, crossing her arms over her chest. "Do you really think phase two is necessary?"

I raise an eyebrow. I detect a note of hesitation in her voice and it sends a thrill of triumph through my system. "This from the woman who accused me of not being willing to do what's necessary? Now that you see I am, you're worried I'll succeed." I watch her face for tells, but there's something in her eyes that doesn't seem to agree with my assessment. There's a reluctance I've never noticed before. Perhaps the implications of her part in phase two have finally sunk in. "You're afraid. It's all well and good for you to sit back and whisper in Jade's ear that I'm not capable of going far enough, but when it comes down to it, you're the one who can't do what it takes."

Lena draws her shoulders back and lifts her chin. "That's not it. I'm just wondering if there isn't another way. How do you even know it'll come to phase two?"

"Of course it will," I say dismissively. I thought long and hard about this plan and how to ensure its success. There can be no loopholes, no hope left for Krissa. "You don't know her as I do. Believe me, this is the only way to gain her unwavering allegiance. Now, unless you want to be the one to explain to Jade how you're responsible for us not having an assassin, get back into position."

A shadow flickers across Lena's face. I'm sure she wants to argue—I sense it's in her nature—but she seems to think better of it. Without another word, she slips into her car and drives back down the road in the direction from which she came.

I could get used to people taking my orders like that. In fact, I plan to grow quite accustomed to it. If Lena continues to give me the respect I deserve, I might be able to turn her loyalty to my advantage. Despite how annoying she can be, her spark could benefit my new administration. Her spirit is one that, once tamed, could be of use to me.

Chapter Thirty-Four
Krissa

I've been drumming my fingers against my thigh for the last ten minutes. This is taking too long. There's only half an hour remaining before Brody's deadline.

Lexie sits in the driver's seat of Felix's car while he calls out directions based on the impressions he's receiving through his makeshift dowsing rod. So far, Felix has led us to Hannah's Herbs, Anya's apartment, and Ruby Riddell's house. I suppose I can understand why: The shop is full of elements that can be used in magic—plus, Jodi is a witch, and she's working today. Ruby Riddell—Fox's grandmother—and Anya are both psychics, which could explain why Felix was picking up impressions from each of them.

I can't hold his mistakes against him. He's never attempted this before. It's not his fault he's being forced to practice when the stakes are so high.

We're probably seven minutes from Griffin's apartment, which is where I left my car. If I speed, it might be possible to get to the lonely road where I know Brody is waiting in less than fifteen. I can't afford the luxury of patience anymore. If I want to save Owen and Fox, I know what I need to do. I'm just not sure how to convince Felix and Lexie to let me do it.

With each passing moment, I'm more aware of the pressure of the Influence on my mind, but there's still a kind of wall between me and it. I can't access its power. It's as if the Influence senses chaos somewhere nearby. Like it wants to be a part of it. But the dissevering spell is still holding, and there's no danger of it usurping control of my body.

Felix calls out a direction that will take us even farther from Griffin's house. If I'm going to make my case, I need to do it now; otherwise it'll take too long to get to Brody. I open my mouth, but before I can speak, my phone buzzes. A quick glance reveals a text from Dana. Tears prickle my eyes as relief swells within me. "They think they found Fox."

Lexie and Felix cheer, but my fingers are already flying. "I'm telling them not to rescue him yet." My mind spins with new possibilities, ones I wouldn't let myself consider before. But now that Fox has been found, it changes everything.

Lexie pulls the car over, parking in front of a squat single-story house. "Why?" she asks, turning to face me.

"We don't know who's watching," I say as I press the "send" button. Different scenarios unfold in my head—all the ways things could go wrong. "You'll have to time everything right because we won't get a second chance. It's possible Brody set traps—or if he hasn't, he might have sensors or something, and he could retaliate against Owen if he realizes he can't use Fox as leverage anymore."

Felix also turns in his seat. "Okay, I'll bite. What's the plan?"

I purse my lips. I'd love to give him the information he wants, but I'm still working everything out in my head. Besides, if there's any chance of this working at all, time is of the essence. "I'll let you know. All you need to do right now is take me to my car."

Lexie's brow furrows. "Tell me where you need to go, and I'll drop you."

I've already played out that scenario in my mind. Yes, it would be the fastest option, but the room for unintended consequences grows exponentially by bringing two more people I care about so close to Brody. "No. I have to go alone. I'm going to tell Brody I've made my decision."

For a beat, they both stare at me. Understanding dawns on Felix's face first; a sneaky smile spreads across Lexie's face a second later.

I sigh, thankful when they don't ask me to spell things out for them. "Join up with the others and wait until I tell you it's okay to move on Fox."

"I don't like the idea of you going by yourself," Felix says.

"Not up for discussion."

Lexie and Felix exchange glances. It's obvious neither of them is comfortable with me facing Brody without backup. I understand, but we don't have much of a choice. Felix nods. "Okay, but we don't need to waste time taking you back to your car. Just take mine. I'll have West or someone come get us."

Affection rises within me as I climb out of Felix's car. No sooner is he out than I wrap my arms around him, hugging him as tightly as I can. I hope he understands I'm not just thanking him for the use of his car. His friendship has meant so much to me, and his trust now may help me undo whatever evil Brody has planned.

Felix kisses my forehead. "Be safe," he murmurs as we release each other.

I start for the driver's side of the car, passing Lexie on the way. She holds out the keys, and when I take them, I pause to squeeze her fingers. She returns the pressure and offers a weak smile.

Once I slide back into the car, I don't look at either of them. I'm afraid of what I might see on their faces. It's possible this plan will go sideways. I'd go so far as to say it's likely. But it's the only plan I have. I just have to hope my friends are able to get to Fox without getting hurt themselves.

I point Felix's car in Brody's direction and drive away.

Chapter Thirty-Five
Brody

There are sixteen minutes left before my deadline when I catch sight of the approaching car. It's not Krissa's, but I know it's her behind the wheel. Like I told Lena, I've grown to know her well. She no doubt spent all the time she safely could attempting to find the boys, but locater spells won't work. Even if she tried to summon them, the effect of the magic wouldn't reach either of them due to the enchantments Lena and I cast. She must have finally realized none of her friends' magical attempts stand a chance of saving Owen or Fox. As I knew she would.

She pulls the car to a stop in front of me and climbs out. It looks vaguely familiar—I'm pretty sure it belongs to one of her friends, but I can't remember which. Not that it matters. It isn't as if any of her friends will play much of a role in her life after today. "I see you've finally come to your senses."

She glares, crossing her arms over her chest. "I don't really have a choice, do I? My friends and I have done everything we can think of, but we haven't been able to find Fox or Owen. But this isn't news to you. You knew I'd fail."

I hold my hands up innocently. "I admit, the game wasn't fair. But neither is life." I pause, savoring the moment. Until now, I haven't let myself fantasize too much about how I'll be received when I return to the Amaranthine, new assassin at my side. Jade will, of course, be suitably impressed. Any doubts she may have had about my ability to lead our people will fade away, and she'll give me her unwavering support as her successor. I've always been popular, but when I return victorious, I can't imagine there will be one woman who will turn down any advance I'll make. And then, a few months from now, when I am affirmed as the new high priest, no one will be able to stand against me or my people as I lead us to the immortality we've dreamt of for so long. "So, you'll be my assassin?"

Krissa drops her arms and squares her shoulders. "No."

The images dancing in my mind evaporate. "No? I don't think you understand what that means for your boyfriends."

Her posture doesn't change, and her expression borders on haughty. "I know what it means. I've made my decision. I choose Owen."

My eyebrows hitch upward. Typically, I'm able to keep a poker face, but her decision is unexpected. "You realize that if you choose Owen —"

"Fox dies. I know." The briefest flicker of hesitation crosses her face, but she blinks it away. "I don't want it to happen, but it's what I have to choose. I can't go with you. I won't give into the Influence and be your assassin. I told you, I'll never stop fighting for the future I deserve. Owen doesn't trust me after what happened with Fox. If Fox is gone..." She squeezes her eyes shut and her lips tremble. "If he's gone, Owen won't ever have to doubt me again. He'll understand how much I love him."

I scrutinize her face, looking for tells that she's trying to deceive me. There are hints of fear and regret in her eyes, but mostly they're filled with grim determination. My lips curl into a smile. "You're even more heartless than I imagined. I didn't think you were capable of sacrificing someone's life for your own happiness."

"Are you going to honor your original terms or not?" she asks, a hard edge to her voice. "I choose Owen." She checks the screen of her phone. "In thirteen minutes, Fox..." She struggles to swallow before she can continue. "Fox dies. And you leave town forever. Do we have a deal?"

"Of course," I say, keeping my voice light and easy. "I am a man of my word." I sweep my hand toward my car. "I'll take you to Owen."

Her eyebrows scrunch together and seconds pass before she moves. I can't help smiling to myself as she walks toward the car. Not many people can surprise me, but she just did. Although I won't admit it to Lena—or anyone else—this isn't the choice I imagined Krissa would make. I figured there was no way she could live with herself if she allowed someone to die.

Careful not to let her see, I slip my phone from my pocket and tap out a quick message to Lena. *Initiate phase two.*

Chapter Thirty-Six
Krissa

It's taking all of my concentration not to let Brody see how nervous I am. To keep from fidgeting, I sit on my hands. Pinning them beneath my thighs also keeps me from indulging my other urge—checking my phone.

Before I arrived at the meeting place, I sent instructions to the psychics and witches. I told them to scout the perimeter and look for any Amaranthine who might be stationed to make sure no one interferes with Brody's plan. While I haven't seen Brody interacting with anyone, it doesn't mean he is without assistants. My friends will also need to try to figure out if there are any traps that might hurt one of them—or Fox—when they go to save him.

They will save him. I have to believe it. Despite what I said to Brody, I won't let Fox die.

They know I'm with Brody now. The next message I receive should be someone assuring me Fox is safe.

I refuse to allow my mind to dwell on any other scenarios.

I'm surprised when Brody pulls to the side of the road. We've barely traveled a mile from where I met him. We're still on the outskirts of town, where most of the land is dominated by fields of corn or beans, but on this particular plot of land, there are trees. It's not a forest by any stretch of the imagination, but the wooded area covers about half an acre. Plenty of room to hide Owen.

Wordlessly, Brody leads the way into the woods. My heartbeat increases with each step, to the point that I'm afraid Brody might be able to hear it. Does he know I plan to double-cross him? I don't want to think of how he'll react when he finds out.

If he finds out. It's possible he will simply leave town after he takes me to Owen and never learn of my deception. After all, he claims to be a man of his word.

Still, I can't help the sinking feeling in my stomach. No matter what he claims, he wants me to be the assassin, and I can't imagine he'll give up easily.

I shake my head, trying to clear it. I'll deal with the consequences later. All that matters right now is saving Owen and Fox.

Brody slows and turns to me. "He's just ahead in a small clearing." He regards me in a way that makes me feel like he can read my mind. Even though he's not a psychic, I clear my head of any thoughts of Fox or the future, filling it instead with excitement about seeing Owen. "There are few people in this world who have ever managed to best me, Krissa Barnette. You should be honored you can count yourself among them."

My lip curls. Of all the things I could possibly find gratifying, I can't imagine anything less appealing. Still, I don't want to offend him, so I hastily try to make my face look neutral. "Thank you for holding up your end of the deal."

His face tightens for a split second before he shakes his head. "Of course." He takes a few steps back, moving so he's closer to where we came from than I am. "Enjoy your happily ever after."

"I will."

I wait until Brody turns and starts walking away before continuing toward the clearing. He was right—it is small, barely the size of our living room and dining room together. In the center is Owen, his hands bound to a stake in the ground. He's on his knees with his back to me, and he jumps when I release a relieved yelp and run to him.

"You're okay," I say, suddenly breathless. I kneel beside him and my fingers immediately go to the knots binding him. "I was so afraid. We couldn't find you. I don't know what I would've done if they hadn't found Fox." The words tumble from my mouth so quickly I'm not sure Owen can decipher them. "Actually, I know what I would've done. I would've gone with him. I would've gone with Brody to save you."

"It's not too late."

Owen's voice is so flat, so emotionless, that it startles me. As my fingers loosen the last knot, I glance up at his face for the first time. What I see makes my breath catch. He's not pleased to see me. If anything, he looks angry. But that doesn't make any sense. Surely he understands what would've happened if I hadn't found him. Was my mention of Fox enough to erase any trace of relief that he's no longer in danger of dying?

"Are you okay?" I ask, reaching up to stroke his face.

He pulls away before my fingers make contact. "Why did you even bother to come for me?"

"You're not making any sense." An icy thrill of dread shoots down my spine. Something's wrong. Did Brody do something to him? Did he cast some kind of spell to make him act this way? "If I didn't come, Brody was going to kill you."

"And you just couldn't let him do that, could you? No, of course not. Not the great Krissa Barnette. Always right there." He snaps his fingers sharply, making me jump. "Right on the spot to save whoever's in danger." He presses his hands into the grass and pushes himself to his feet. "Don't think I don't know that's the real reason you're here. I know you think you're here because you love me, but you've already proven you're incapable of love."

His words hit me like a sucker punch. I stand and try to move into his line of sight. I know he's upset with me after finding out about Fox. He has every right to be. But this doesn't sound like him. Perhaps Brody has cast some sort of charm to confuse him. "I know you're mad at me and I get it—I do. You think I betrayed you, but I didn't, Owen. If you let me explain, you'll see I never did anything to hurt you. It was all the Influence."

"That's a lie, and we both know it," he snarls. "If you had no feelings for him, you wouldn't have been drawn to him. But you did—you do. You've never been able to convince me you don't." He narrows his eyes and looks at me as if I am something repulsive he found on the bottom of his shoe. "I can see it in your eyes. You want to forget it ever happened and move past it. But I can't. I won't. I want nothing to do with you. As far as I'm concerned, you might as well leave and never come back. I hate you."

I feel as if the wind has been knocked out of me. I can barely take in a breath. Is it possible this is really Owen talking? Is this what he really feels? I thought he could come to terms with what I did when he realized it wasn't really me. But he's never looked at me this way before—not even when I first found myself in this reality and he saw me as nothing more than the girl who broke his heart to join Crystal Jamison's clique.

Pressure builds in my mind as the Influence tests the barrier keeping it in place. There are too many raw emotions flowing through me, too much adrenaline and fear, and it's weakening the wall built by the dissevering spell. But I'm still in control. I can't let it out—I won't. I need to calm down. I need to get Owen to come with me. Felix's car isn't far, and I'll feel much safer once we're nearer to civilization. "Let's get out of here. We don't have to talk, but I don't like the idea of staying here. I don't think Brody will try anything, but it's best not to tempt fate."

"I'm not going anywhere with you," Owen snaps.

We don't have time for this. I filter through different ideas in my head. Maybe I could have someone else pick him up—Lexie or Bria. I get the feeling he wouldn't be too keen on getting in the car with Felix or Tucker at the moment.

He's edging toward the tree line in the opposite direction of the road. I dart forward and close my hand around his wrist, tugging him to a stop.

"Don't touch me! Don't ever lay your hands on me again."

I release him and step back, afraid he might strike out at me. I've never seen such loathing in anyone's eyes before. I didn't even think Owen was capable of that kind of hatred. "I don't know what's going on, but this isn't you. Something's wrong. You don't have to let me help you, but let me bring you to someone who can."

"Krissa!"

I jump at the sound of my name. The voice came from behind me, but my brain is having trouble figuring out how it's possible. It's Owen's voice—but Owen is standing in front of me. At first I think I must be imagining things, but when I hear my name again, I turn.

Someone is approaching the clearing, but it can't be who I think it is. It must be my mind playing tricks on me—too much adrenaline or not enough oxygen or something. But when the figure crosses through the last of the trees and steps into the sunlight, I can't deny what my eyes are seeing. Owen stands, his hair a mess, a vivid red gash across his cheek, looking relieved to have found me. "Get away from her!" he calls. "You can't trust anything he says. They had me tied up, but I escaped. Brody's trying to trick you. That's not me, Krissa! It's not me."

I stand, frozen in place, not sure what to do. Can the person in front of me really be Owen? But if he is, who have I been talking to? Trepidation laces with curiosity as I twist to look at the person behind me. For a moment, it still appears to be Owen, but then the image shifts before my eyes. The Owen behind me begins to shimmer and melt away until all that remains is a woman I've never seen before. She's short—probably no taller than I am—with brown hair and green eyes. She wears a red tank top, jeans, and a haughty expression.

A smile stretches across the woman's face. "I'll admit, he's more resourceful than I anticipated." She glances past me toward Owen—the real Owen. "How did you manage to get away?"

My mind reels, struggling to make sense of what's happening. "What's going on here? Why were you pretending to be Owen?"

"Isn't it obvious?" the woman asks, her tone indicating she thinks it ought to be. But nothing is obvious right now—everything is twisted and it's making my brain hurt. The Influence continues to push against my consciousness, and I have to focus now to keep it from breaking through.

"It's Brody," Owen says. "He's desperate for you to be his assassin. He figured if you thought I hated you, you'd think there was nothing left for you in Clearwater and go with him."

"But it didn't work," the woman growls. "I told him it wouldn't. You can't just think there's nothing left for you—there actually has to *be* nothing left for you."

Before I can work out what she might mean by that, she conjures a handful of something like crackling blue lightning and throws it toward Owen. He calls out in pain and I rush to him.

He's on the ground. Whatever she hit him with knocked him over. "You okay?"

He grimaces. "I've been better."

The woman shoots another spell in our direction, and it narrowly misses Owen. I position myself between him and her. I can't use magic to protect him, so I bank on how much Brody wants me. I can only hope his desire for me to be the assassin is enough to keep this woman from hurting me to get to Owen.

I curse myself for not having prepared for a double-cross from Brody. Of course things weren't going to be this easy. I should have known better than to trust him on any level.

Another bolt of blue electricity tears up the ground by my feet. "We have to get out of here. Can you move?"

Owen tries to get to his feet, but the color drains from his face and he tumbles back to the ground. "You have to leave me. Go get help."

"No," I say firmly. "I'm going to get us both out of here."

I mean the words as a promise, but I have no idea how I'll fulfill them. Without the Influence, I have no kind magic to combat the attack, and in Owen's current state, I don't think his psychic abilities will be much help. The only thing I know for sure is that I'm going to save the person I love most of all, no matter the cost.

Chapter Thirty-Seven
Fox

I can't gauge how long I've been out here. It feels like forever, but the sun barely seems to have moved overhead. I'm sure it's my adrenaline making time seem to slow down. My whole body trembles with the energy to attack or run to safety. I wonder how long a body can stay working properly with stress hormones coursing through it. It has to be longer than I've been tied up here, but I don't see how.

My throat hurts and I'm pretty sure I've shouted myself hoarse. Even though I know there are spells cast around me to keep my voice from carrying, I can't help calling out every time I see a car, on the off chance I break through.

I've tried every spell I can think of to loosen the knots around my wrist, to send up some kind of signal alerting passersby to my whereabouts, to break the pole I'm attached to so I can run to the street, but nothing has worked. It's like whatever's concealing me is also canceling out my magic.

Even though I know my spells won't work and my shouts won't carry, I can't stop trying. If I do, I'll start thinking about what's going to happen to me. As hard as I try to keep them at bay, possible outcomes continue to pop into my head.

I'm pretty sure I'm going to die.

The woman made it sound like that's what's going to happen. She said I wouldn't be around long. I highly doubt she was referring to some fabulous vacation she has planned for me.

If it's true, I wish there were some way I could leave a message— some last words. I want to say something to my dad and Griffin, of course. I'd tell them to make peace, to get along for my sake—and for Mom's. I'd leave a message for Dana, too. I'd apologize for hurting her the way I did. It was shitty of me to lie, no matter my reasons. I'd tell her she's a good person who deserves way better than what I've put her through.

I wish I could go back and make different decisions about the whole Krissa thing. The first time she approached me, weeks ago, I was afraid to say or do anything to make her regret telling me about the feelings she still had for me. I didn't want to give her any reason not to be with me. But I should've been stronger—I should've told her I wouldn't be with her if we had to lie. How messed up is that? What does it mean about me that if I could go back and change things, I'd still be with her, even though I know without a doubt Owen is the one she really wants?

Before I can dwell on it too long, a noise attracts my attention. There's a muffled sound coming from behind me, but no matter how hard I twist, I can't turn far enough to see what's making it.

I take in a deep breath and steel myself for the inevitable. This must be it—the end. I don't know what the woman has in mind for my demise, but I'm sure it has to do with magic. I do my best not to imagine in too much detail what could be making the muffled sounds. Is it a spell of some kind? Or a machine? Or has she somehow enchanted wild animals to do her bidding?

My heart thunders in my chest and I squeeze my eyes closed, waiting for my death, but it doesn't come. Seconds tick by, and the muffled sounds grow no louder. Instead, it feels as if weights are being lifted from my chest one by one. My breaths come easier. I wasn't even aware it was harder to breathe than usual until whatever was pressing down on me was removed.

In addition to the muffled sounds, new sounds meet my ears.

Birds chirping. Traffic in the distance. And voices.

That's Griffin's voice—and Dana's.

Footfalls sound, getting closer and closer to my position until people come into view. There's Griffin and Dana—and they are joined by the whole circle and all the psychics, save Krissa and Owen. Even Sasha hovers by my side.

Fingers dig into my wrists as someone tries to loosen the ropes that are binding me. As soon as they fall, Griffin pulls me into a hug so tight I can't breathe again. I'm so surprised I don't return it right away. We're not exactly a hugging family—I think the last time Griffin embraced me like this may have been when our mom died.

"Don't you ever scare me like that again, you hear?" Griffin murmurs fiercely in my ear.

"I won't," I promise, even though it's one I know I can't possibly keep. But it's the only thing I can say right now to make him feel better, and somehow there's nothing I want more.

When Griffin releases me, I survey the others. Everyone's faces show a mix of happiness and relief—everyone but Sasha. She stands just outside our group, her brow knit with concern.

"That was too easy," she says, her voice low as if she's afraid to be overheard.

Lexie and Bria exchange glances. "You call that easy?" Lexie asks.

"That was some of the hardest spellwork I've ever had to do to break those enchantments," Crystal says.

Sasha waves a hand. "I get that, but look around. There's no one here to stop us. There are no traps. Hell, there's not even a bomb or something to do Fox in."

"Hey!" Griffin snaps, suddenly defensive.

A heavy feeling of dread settles in my stomach. "So what are you saying?"

Sasha presses her lips together. "I'm not even sure. This just... It feels like a setup."

West's posture straightens and he looks around as if preparing for an attack. "You think we're in danger?"

She shakes her head. "No. I think Krissa is. We have to figure out where they're keeping Owen."

Chapter Thirty-Eight
Krissa

Pain ricochets up my leg and through my body when a bolt of the blue lightning hits me. So far, the woman has been circling us, trying to get a good angle on Owen, but it seems she's growing impatient. Maybe I'm not as important as I think I am.

"Can you use your telekinesis to shield us?" It's a long shot, but Owen's powers might be the only thing that can keep us safe until I'm able to formulate a plan.

His face is tight with pain. "I can try." He closes his eyes like he's trying to concentrate. More electricity comes our way, but this time it's deflected.

I'm so happy I almost shout with relief. If Owen can keep this up, it's possible I can drag him through the woods until we get to the road. And if I can get a message off to our friends, someone could be waiting there to get us when we emerge.

"Okay, I'm going to try to drag you. I'm sorry in advance if this hurts." I do my best not to worry whether Owen's protective bubble will hold as I move behind him and hook my arms under his shoulders. I start tugging him and he winces and groans as he slides over the ground. From this angle, I can see where the spell impacted him. It scorched through his green T-shirt and an angry red burn is visible on his stomach. Looking away from it, I grit my teeth and try pulling him again.

This isn't going to work. He's too heavy for me, and there's no way I'll be able to navigate over the bumpy terrain once we get into the trees. I need another plan, but there's no time. Blast after blast of blue lightning flies our way, and I flinch each time. I don't know how we're going to get away. If the spell surrounding this location has been broken, it's possible the others could find us, but are they even looking? I assured them I'd be able to save Owen, that they only needed to concern themselves with Fox.

"I'm going to call for help," I say, releasing Owen and pulling my phone out.

A voice in the back of my mind tells me there's another way—a quicker and easier way—but I ignore it. The pressure of the Influence on my consciousness grows with each passing moment. I'm afraid if it gets much stronger it could drive me mad, or make my head explode. It wants out even more now that there's a battle going on. But I can't let it, because letting it out means trapping me behind that wall, and I can't risk that.

My thumb slides over the screen of my phone, unlocking it, but before I can place a call, a jolt of electricity knocks it from my hand. My yelp of surprise is nothing compared to the sound that comes from Owen as a second wave hits him in the arm.

He's not strong enough to keep a shield around us.

Instinctively, I put myself between him and our attacker.

"We have to run," Owen says through gritted teeth. "Once we're in the woods, maybe we can find somewhere to hide."

"You can't move," I say, remembering the last time he tried to get to his feet.

He shakes his head stubbornly. "Think I've got enough adrenaline to get me going. It's our only shot."

Pain sears through my shoulder as I'm struck again. Owen's right: The only chance we have is to put some distance between us and this madwoman. "Okay."

"On three," he says.

I nod. "One. Two. Three!"

To my great surprise, Owen's able to get his feet under him. When we start running, he keeps pace with me. We're going to make it. Calling for help with my phone isn't an option anymore, but maybe the adrenaline will give Owen enough of a boost to enable him to contact one of the psychics with his abilities. All we'll need to do is lie low until help arrives.

I'm nearly to the trees when Owen releases a scream of agony. By the time I turn, he's already on the ground.

I know it's bad before I make it to his side. Although he was hit in the back, the energy must have gone straight through his body. There's a new whole in his shirt and the wound is visible on his chest. She must have decided she's done playing, because this hit is worse than any of the ones we've taken so far.

I crouch beside him, and Owen's eyes find my face. "You need to get out of here," he says, his voice weak.

I blink, and hot tears stream down my face. His face is ghostly pale and his fingers are trembling. "I won't leave you."

"I can't let you die for me."

A sob bubbles up through my chest and I struggle not to release it. He can't let me die for him—but isn't that exactly what he's doing for me now? Because there's no doubt in my mind Owen is dying. There's blood, though not nearly as much as I would have imagined. His damaged skin is charred black and his breaths are coming in gasps.

This is my fault. It's all my fault. The only reason Owen is here at all is that he has the misfortune of being loved by me. I thought the danger to him was the darkness inside me after I killed Seth, and then I feared the Influence would do something to hurt him, but now I know better: just being around me has put his life in danger.

"If you're going to say your goodbyes, I recommend you do it quickly," calls the woman from behind me. I'd almost forgotten she was there. "I've never seen someone last long after hit like that."

I turn to glare at her. "Why did you do it? What could you

possibly get out of killing him?"

"I was aiming for you," she says easily. "You should hear Brody going on and on about what a perfect assassin you'll make for us. And the high priestess eats it up. He's her favored child who can do no wrong. And she sent me here to help him." She tips back her head and lets out a laugh that makes the hairs on my arms stand up. "Can you imagine? As if I would do anything to help him. I want to see him fail. He doesn't deserve to be our leader, and I'm going to show everyone how wrong they are about him. If I kill you, he loses everything."

"Is that what this is about? Some play for power?" I shake my head. I don't even care. It doesn't matter—nothing matters except Owen. I turn back to him and my heart aches. His breaths are more ragged than before and his eyes are going glassy. He doesn't have much time left.

This insane woman wants me dead? Fine. Then this is how I'll die. I'm done fighting. I don't want to live anymore, not if my whole life is destined to be a series of events like this. How much more can I lose? My life could go on without Owen, but do I want it to?

He lifts a shaking hand and I clasp it. His lips move like he's trying to say something, but no sound comes out. I lean closer, hoping to catch his words, but it's no use. The strength is leaving his hand.

I lock my eyes on his. "I love you." I press my lips to his, tasting the salt of my tears. A moment later, his mouth goes slack, and when I meet his eyes again, I know he's gone.

"Do it," I call, keeping my eyes on his face. Even if I somehow managed to get away, this woman would just come after me. And if not her, someone else—Brody trying to make me his assassin, or some as-yet-unknown entity wanting something from me. I never signed up for any of this. I only ever wanted a normal life, but it seems fate never had one in the cards for me. Faces float in my mind's eye—my mom, Jodi, my dad. All my friends—Felix, Griffin,

Tucker, Lexie. But I can't think about them. I can't worry what my death will do to them when it's painfully obvious my life is the real problem. If I choose to go on, how long will it be until someone decides to use one of them against me? I can't have any more blood on my hands.

"Aren't you even going to turn to face me?"

I ignore her. I curl forward, resting my cheek on Owen's chest. A fresh wave of tears fills my eyes when I don't detect even the slightest rising and falling there. I'm ready.

An explosion goes off in my head, so intense and violent I'm sure I must be dying, sure she must have aimed her spell at my skull. But I'm not dying. I'm on my feet. Time seems to slow. I watch as the blue electricity sails through the air toward me and I raise my palm between me and it. It freezes in midair before disappearing, leaving behind the barest wisp of smoke.

Every inch of my body is on fire with the familiar burn of Influence. I fight to win control, but nothing I can do makes my arms or legs obey. I watch what's happening, like a passenger catching glimpses out the windows of my own eyes. My hand slashes through the air and the woman's tank top splits open from just below her rib cage on one side to just above her hip on the other. A split second later, blood blossoms out of the open wound, soaking the red fabric surrounding it, causing it to glisten in the sunlight. Her eyes go wide—perfect circles of surprise. In another second, she crumples to the ground, her eyes still open but unseeing.

The immediate danger contained, the Influence dials back in intensity from a raging fire to a low simmer. Sensing a chance, my consciousness lunges forward in an attempt to take control of my body once more. For the moment, the wall between me and the Influence is weakened, but I don't know how long it will last. If it goes back up and I'm on the wrong side of it, who knows what could happen.

But maybe having access to the Influence isn't such a bad thing—at least for the moment. When I talked to Jodi about stopping my heart, she warned that bringing someone back from death was dark magic. But what is darker than the Influence inside me? Maybe one good thing can come from the evil sharing my body. I have to try.

I turn, ready to attempt to wield the Influence on Owen, but his body is gone. But it can't be. He was just here. Right here. Where could he have disappeared to? Did I move when the Influence took over? I search the ground, but he's nowhere in sight. There's only one body in the clearing, and it belongs to that woman.

I turn my gaze in her direction, but what I see doesn't make any sense. The woman had been wearing a tank top, but the person lying on the ground now is in a T-shirt. A green T-shirt. My mind struggles to make sense of what I'm seeing. That's where she was standing—I'm positive. Then why doesn't it look like her?

I stumble forward in jerky steps, my heart twisting and sinking with each step.

It's not the woman.

It's Owen.

Bile rises in my throat and I retch on the grass, but I can't unsee the slash across his abdomen, the blood shimmering in the sunshine.

It was all a trick—some kind of illusion cast to confuse me. For all I know, the woman I thought I killed doesn't even exist. Instead, my spell hit Owen.

I crawl to his side, desperate to find something—anything—to indicate my eyes are deceiving me. I press my fingers to his neck, hoping to detect some trace of life, but no blood surges beneath my touch. This can't be real, but I can't deny what I'm seeing.

I turn and vomit again until it feels like there's nothing left inside me. What have I done? What have I done?

There's movement in my periphery. Brody enters the clearing, a look of smug satisfaction on his face. Without warning, the Influence surges forward with such ferocity I stand no chance of beating it back. The burning beneath my skin seems to extend until a ball of fire hovers above my outstretched palm. Brody deserves to die. He orchestrated all of this. I want nothing more than to throw this fire at him, to incinerate him.

But I don't want to kill him—not really. I don't want any more blood on my hands, even Brody's. I can't give in to the Influence. I focus all my energy on keeping my hand still. I can't make the fireball disappear, but I can keep myself from throwing it.

"This was your plan all along, wasn't it?" I ask.

Brody holds up his hands, but not in a way that suggests he surrenders, or that he is even the slightest bit afraid of what I could do to him. Instead, it's a show of mock innocence that makes my fingers twitch with the desire to end him.

"I didn't make you do anything. I simply allowed you to find your true self. You've been trying to fight it for some time, but you're a killer in your bones and you know it. It's not just the Influence. You stabbed Seth through the heart without it; you could have gotten away from Kai without blowing him to pieces—but you didn't. Don't you see what I've done here? I've set you free. Now you can be you really are without anything holding you back."

I stare at the fire in my hand. I could easily launch it at Brody. I want to. But wouldn't that prove his point? It's true, I felt the darkness in me long before the Influence spell. It's part of who I am. And Brody doesn't even know everything. He doesn't know about the time I conjured a fireball so large it nearly stole the air from the room the witches were in because I thought they'd tried to kill Felix. Maybe Brody's right. Maybe I've been pretending for too long that I'm normal, but that's really not what I am. It's not who I am.

The Influence surges forward again as if in agreement. Was it fate that brought the Influence to me? I knew what having it inside me would mean, but I let it in anyway. I tried to tell myself I was saving Crystal and Dana, but what if I was really saving myself? What if altering the timeline and releasing Seth and connecting with Owen, what if Sasha contacting Brody, what if everything that happened since I moved to Clearwater was all orchestrated to lead to this moment? What if this is who I was meant to be all along?

My eyes drift from the fireball to Owen's lifeless body and grief swells in my chest. If that's true, was Owen always meant to die by my hand? I don't know if I can live with that.

Maybe I don't have to.

I'm growing weaker by the second as I fight against the Influence. Just moments ago I realized I don't want my life to be a series of struggles leading only to heartache. Maybe it's time to give up.

I allow my consciousness to stop struggling against the Influence. Once I let go, my ego, my self, sinks down into the depths of my mind, and waves of the Influence crash over me.

***

I close my hand and the fireball disappears. I roll my shoulders and stretch out my fingers. This is more like it. No more vying for control or straining for dominance. This is the way it should have been from the beginning, but that silly girl fought me. In all my various incarnations, I've never encountered anyone so set against letting me in and allowing me to use my full power. But that won't be a problem anymore. *She* won't be a problem anymore.

To my left is the body of the boy she loved—the dull one who bored me with his devotion. He was so concerned, so considerate. I never understood his allure. I much preferred the other boy I found in the depths of her memories. Fox. He didn't hesitate for a moment the night I showed up at his door, even though I know for a fact his girlfriend had left only minutes before. He claimed the deception made him uncomfortable, but it never stopped him from being with me. Far more interesting.

In front of me stands Brody of the Amaranthine. I've known of his group for many years, but I've never had occasion to meet someone from it. Their reputation is somewhat fearsome, but now I can't help wondering if it's not a little overblown. I can smell Brody's fear. It's pungent—fear for both his physical body and for something else, something deeper. His gaze is locked on mine with an unwavering intensity, and his muscles are taut, prepared for flight at a moment's notice.

Adorable. It's always the ones who make others fear them and bend to their wills who understand instinctively when they're out of their depth. He may have been the master puppeteer with the old Krissa Barnette, but his tricks won't work on me.

"You can relax," I murmur. I take a step forward and Brody fights to keep still and not flinch. My lips curl into a smile. "You were right—what you were saying before. This whole setup you orchestrated has set me free. Unlike that silly girl, I would love to fill the role you've offered. Assassin sounds like the perfect job for someone of my... appetites."

Brody visibly relaxes, tension draining from his shoulders as he releases a breath. "That's exactly what I like to hear. Now, let's get going."

I smile, leading the way out of the clearing. "Let's."

Chapter Thirty-Nine
Fox

I ignore Griffin's shouts as I jump out of his Mustang before he's even pulled it to a complete stop. The psychics have been dowsing for magic and they all got strong sensations radiating from this spot.

This has to be where Owen is, and if he's here, so is Krissa.

I'm jogging into the small wooded area before the last of the cars even arrive. There are crashes in the underbrush behind me, so I know I'm not the only one heading in already. I'm not the only one who's worried.

"Be careful," Dana calls from behind me. "You have no idea what you're running into."

I don't look back, but I do slow down. Guilt squeezes my chest like a fist. She still cares about me despite what I've done to her. I don't deserve it, but I won't reject it and hurt her more. Besides, she has a point. The psychics only detected magical energy coming from this area—they didn't identify what was causing it. Who knows what kind of spells or enchantments are at work here.

I wait until the others have caught up with me before venturing further.

"The magic isn't as strong as it was," West says, his voice low. "It's more like echoes."

"I'm not sensing any people," Bria adds.

Panic wells inside me, but I try to stuff it down. Just because

Bria doesn't sense anything doesn't mean something bad has happened. It's possible there are spells at work that would keep a psychic from picking up on a specific presence.

A small hand slips into mine. My first instinct is to pull away. I figure it's Dana, and I'm not worthy of her sympathy. But when I turn, I'm surprised to see Crystal. Her lips twitch like she's trying to offer a smile, but she can't quite make her muscles cooperate. Her blue eyes are full of the same worry that sits in the pit of my stomach.

"She'll be okay," she murmurs.

It's not lost on me that her words sound more like a wish or a prayer than an assurance.

Ahead, the trees begin to thin. We're coming up to a clearing. This has to be where they're keeping Owen.

We all slow our pace as we approach. I glance at the others at the head of the group—Felix, Lexie, West, Tucker—and give a nod. When it's returned, we lead the way through the last of the trees.

I scan the area. It's not particularly large—maybe the size of my basement—but I'm sure I must be missing something. It's empty. But that can't be. They have to be here. Maybe Brody cast a glamor to make them invisible. Something has to explain why I don't see them.

Griffin, Bridget, and Bria surge forward, but when they see what I see—emptiness—their steps falter. Sasha is the only one who continues further into the clearing.

"There was magic here, all right," she says, crouching down beside a deep gouge in the ground. "You can see all the spots where spells got deflected."

When I look around again, I'm surprised I didn't notice the holes and upturned chunks of earth earlier. "It looks like there was some kind of battle." But that doesn't make sense. Even if Krissa intended to come alone to rescue Owen, she's not a witch anymore. She couldn't be casting spells. And it wouldn't explain where she is now.

"Spread out," Sasha says. "Let's try to figure out what happened here. Tell me if you find anything."

We all do as instructed, but I have no idea what I'm looking for. There are a few scorch marks in the grass near me, but they give no insight into what went down or why.

"I found something," Bridget calls. She's kneeling in a spot near the center of the clearing. "It's a stake. And there are ropes. This must be where he was tied."

Bria crouches and holds her hand over the spot. "Definitely. I can feel his energy."

I wait for more information, but Bria doesn't seem to have any. "So what? We already figured he was here. Where is he now? What happened?" A survey of my companions reveals nothing but shrugs and upturned palms.

"I may have something," Sasha calls. She's on her hands and knees a few feet away, scrutinizing a patch of grass. "I think someone was lying down over here."

After a moment, Felix asks the obvious question. "Why would someone be lying down? Were they hurt?"

"I can't tell," she says, not looking up. "I don't see any blood. But this looks like..." She leans down farther and sniffs a spot gingerly before yanking her head away. "Yeah, that's vomit."

The mention of the word makes bile rise in my throat. What could have happened to make someone throw up? Was it Krissa?

Sasha stands up and brushes her hands on her thighs. Griffin takes a step toward her. "So, where are they?"

Her eyebrows hitch upward like she's surprised by the question. "I have no idea. I've already told you everything I know: There's some vomit. Someone was lying there, but I don't know why. It doesn't appear that anyone got dragged away, so maybe whoever was lying down got up and walked off. I don't know. The only thing I'm pretty sure of is that Owen and Krissa were here, but they're not anymore."

"Do you think she went with him?" Dana asks, her voice small. "Brody wanted her to be his new assassin—and if there's one thing I learned about Brody, it's that he doesn't give up until he gets what he wants."

Silence settles over the group. I'm sure we're all thinking it, but no one wants to be the one to say it. What if Brody did something to make Krissa agree to join him? Is it possible she's with him now, on her way to wherever the Amaranthine are to become a weapon for them to point at whoever makes them angry?

There's movement around me. Everyone is heading back into the woods, back to the road, their cars, their lives. Anger surges inside me. Everyone is giving up? We're supposed to admit defeat?

A hand closes over my shoulder. "Come on, Fox," Griffin says, his voice gentle. "Let's get out of here."

I shake my head. "We still haven't figured out what happened. There has to be some kind of clue."

I try to turn away from him, but he doesn't release his grip. "There isn't. And if what Dana said is true, if Krissa really did join the Amaranthine, I don't know if there's anything we can do. I don't think it's the kind of organization you can just leave."

I knock his hand away. "So, what? That's it? She's gone and we just accept it?"

Anger flashes in his eyes, along with something else—something deeper. Pain. The same kind of pain I used to detect when I'd find him in his room, alone, crying about Mom. It's been so long I'd almost forgotten what it's like to see him vulnerable. "I care about her, too, but this might be a battle we can't win. Have you stopped to think that if she went with that douche, it might have been to save your sorry ass? He was going to kill you to make her go with him. Do you think she'd ever let that happen?"

I can't meet his eyes. He's right, but I don't want to admit it. My history with Krissa might be complicated, but one fact is undeniable: She'd do anything to save the people she cares about. She stabbed Seth through the heart to save her father. She gave up her magic and psychic abilities so the Influence would fill her instead of Crystal and Dana. And now, she might have agreed to be an assassin to keep the Amaranthine from coming after me again.

I'm not sure exactly what happened here, but one thing is clear in my mind: I'm going to find Krissa, and I'm going to get her back.

No matter what.

ABOUT THE AUTHOR

Madeline Freeman lives in the metro-Detroit area with her husband, her daughter and son, and her cats. She loves anything to do with astronomy, outer space, plate tectonics, and dinosaurs, and secretly hopes her kids will become astronomers or paleontologists.

Connect with Madeline online:
http://www.madelinefreeman.net
http://twitter.com/writer_maddie
http://facebook.com/madelinefreemanbooks

Sign up for Madeline's reader's group for updates and exclusive content!

https://laurealinde.leadpages.co/mailing-list-signup

CPSIA information can be obtained
at www.ICGtesting.com
Printed in the USA
LVOW11s2318250417
532191LV00001B/186/P

9 781530 469260